Saint's HEAVEN

An Urban Romance

2

A NOVEL BY

SHAMEKA JONES
& VIRGO

CHAPTER 1

Heaven

$\mathcal{I}$ was miserable without Saint, but I was not going to let his insecurities stress me out. He had been gone for a few weeks, and I had cried for every night that he was gone. I was so messed up that my mother offered to come from South Carolina. I turned down the offer, but told her that the boys and I would come visit as soon as school was out. I just needed time to get things in order for me to take a vacation. I had not even reached out to him, but he had not tried to contact me either. I was just blown away that Saint could believe for one minute that I would be that treacherous. As much as I wanted to be "Team Fuck Saint," I loved him. He just needed to get his shit together before we ever had any type of relationship.

To get my mind off Saint, I had been spending time with a couple of the mothers I had met on Facebook. Tressa and Vedra were cool. They definitely brought less drama than Kalina brought to the table. They were like me; about their kids and their money. We had plans to go to dinner. Our kids would be going with us since I did not have a babysitter. I had completely cut Flex off and since Ms. Peggy claimed she did not want to get in the middle of our drama, I cut her ass off too. I loved Ms. Peggy but she had raised a fucked up son, and because of that she was cut off until further notice for the sake of my pregnancy.

"Legend and King! Get your shoes on," I called down the stairs as I struggled to fit into a pair of jeans.

"Okay!" they both yelled back. I doubted it would be done by the time I got downstairs, but I crossed my fingers.

Growing frustrated with my pants not wanting to button, I took them off and started to look for something else to put on. I was starting to get too big for my clothes and was in desperate need of maternity clothes. I had not had it in me to go shopping, but I made a note to do some online shopping when we got home from dinner because I was running out of work clothes as well. I finally decided on a white Dolman sleeved tunic and black leggings that I paired with some ballet flats. I accented the plain black and white with some turquoise jewelry. I left my hair in its naturally curly state so that I looked casual and comfortable.

I was happy when I got downstairs and the kids had their shoes on. They had been dealing with my breakup with Saint pretty well. I hated that the moment I had brought a new man in our lives, he bailed. I did not want my kids thinking that this was okay, so we had a serious conversation. I let them know that even though Saint and I loved each other very much, we did not work in a relationship. That did not mean that I loved them any less, or that they had anything to do with the breakup. I let them know that sometimes adults acted like kids.

"Mama, where are we eating?" Legend asked. He was my picky

eater. All he ever wanted to eat was chicken. It did not matter where we went.

"We're gonna go to Olive Garden," I answered.

"Do they have chicken tenders?"

"Yes L...they do," I laughed as we got in the car.

When we pulled up to the restaurant, Vedra was already waiting outside with her daughter Catana. Catana was the cutest seven-year-old I had ever seen. She was the color of milk chocolate with hazel eyes and deep dimples. Vedra always had her hair in ponytails with huge bows. We joked that we would arrange Catana and King to get married because Catana was bossy toward him, and he did whatever she asked. My baby was a true gentleman.

"I already got us on the list. Tressa is on the way," Vedra said, greeting me with a hug as I sat beside her on the bench she was occupying.

"That's good. I'm starving."

"When are you not starving?" Vedra laughed. "That baby got you eating everything."

"I know, right? All I'm thinking about is my appetizer, dinner, and dessert."

We waited a few minutes more, and Tressa showed up just as the buzzer went off letting us know that our table was ready. Tressa had three kids. She had a fourteen-year-old son named Niqwan, a twelve-year-old daughter name Kimora, and an eleven-year-old daughter named Anika. They all participated in some type of sport, so it was no surprise that they were running late because they had to pick Qwan up from football practice.

"I can't wait till these kids start driving so I can stop playing chauffeur," Tressa said as we sat down for dinner.

"The kids want to get into sports. I might let them this year," I said, looking over my menu.

"Well, be prepared to kiss your weekends goodbye," Tressa said, rolling her eyes. "Especially football."

"You don't have to tell me," I laughed. "I grew up in South Carolina, where football is our religion and the games are revival."

"It's the same way in Texas."

We all laughed. The waitress came and got our drink order while we looked over the menu. By the time she got back, we were ready to order. Dinner was filled with laughter and good conversation. It definitely brought me out of my funk. I had not even thought about Saint. Tressa and Vedra both knew about the situation, but they never spoke on it unless I brought it up. Even then, they were not quick to put in their two cents. They just wanted to get my mind off of things, which was the main purpose of going out to dinner tonight.

"Ya'll ready to go?" Vedra asked as we sat around the table talking. We had just finished dessert and were just enjoying each other's company.

"Yeah. Qwan has football practice in the morning and the girls have cheer," Tressa answered, paying her bill on the tablet on the table. I loved that most restaurants were moving to that technology. We did not have to chase a waiter down for our check.

"I gotta get the boys in bed," I said, noticing King's eyes getting heavy at the table.

We all paid our bills and got up to leave. As we were walking through the restaurant, my eyes landed on the last person I wanted to see. He was with someone too. That shit hit me in my heart to see Saint on a date only weeks after he and I broke up. My hand immediately went to my stomach. I just hoped that no one else saw him because he had not noticed me yet. I just wanted to get out of the restaurant as fast as possible.

"Hey Saint," Legend said from behind me. Saint looked at me like he had seen a ghost.

"Hey little man," Saint said, giving him a pound.

"Come on L…let's go," I said, grabbing him by the hand. King was walking ahead with Vedra and Catana, so he had not noticed Saint.

I tried to speed through the restaurant. I hoped that Saint would not come after me. I could not bear to stand around and have small talk with the man I loved and his date while I was carrying his baby.

"Heav, wait," I heard Saint call me. I tried to walk faster, but he caught up to me easily.

"Vee…can you take Legend and King to the car for a minute," I finally said to Vedra. She looked from me to Saint before nodding and grabbing the keys I was holding out for her.

"What Saint?" I finally said once everyone was out of earshot.

"How have you been feeling?"

"I don't see how that's your concern since you don't think it's your baby," I replied, crossing my arms and resting them on my belly.

"I'm trying to be nice. *If* that is my baby, I want to know that you are taking care of yourself."

That nigga was trying to play me like I was some mindless hood rat off of the street. I just stared at him. I did not know if I wanted to love him or slap him. Here he was on a date with someone else and trying to act like he cared about me at the same time.

"There you go, Saint," the woman he was having dinner with caught up to me. She looked me up and down before holding her hand out. "I'm Lailani...and you are?"

I stared at her hand as if it had the plague on it. She was a beautiful woman, but I could tell that she was one of those spoiled pampered bitches who never worked for a thing a day in her life. She always relied on a man to take care of her. When she realized that I was not going to shake her hand, she placed her other hand on Saint's chest and I saw it. My stomach leaped into my throat when I saw the huge rock on her finger. That negro did not skip a beat.

"Saint, we should get going," she said, taking him by the hand.

I stood there dumbfounded. I watched as he walked off hand in hand with the same bitch that cheated on him twice, but he accused me of cheating. I wanted him to explain to me how he could do it, but I was the one who told him to leave. I was not going to press the issue. If that's who he wanted to be with, then he was welcome to be with her.

CHAPTER 2

Saint

*A*fter staying in hotels for a few weeks, I ended up going to my mother's house. This was the last place that I wanted to be, but I could not keep wasting money on rooms. I started house hunting last week, so I should only be here a few months. She bitched and moaned about that until I finally threw her some cash. My mother was money hungry, she would take money from a homeless person if they had it. That was the main thing that I didn't like about her, especially since she didn't raise me. She always had her hand out begging. At the end of the day, she gave me life, so I owe her a little something.

"Saint!" my mother called out as she opened the bedroom door.

"Yes."

"When you gon' get up and do something? You can't sit and mope around the house all day. That shit is making me depressed."

"What you want me to do?"

"Shit, something besides sitting in this room."

"I don't have anything to do today. Why is my being in this room depressing you?"

"'Cause I'm not used to seeing you like this."

I wanted to tell her she wasn't used to seeing me at all, but I wasn't up for a fight right now.

"I'm getting up now."

"Good 'cause I have company coming over in a lil' while."

She walked out the room, slamming the door behind her. I pulled the covers back over my head and closed my eyes. I didn't see the need of me getting up since she was having company. It's not like they were going to be in here with me.

Since I couldn't fall back to sleep, I got on up. I pulled some clothes from the suitcase I was living out of to iron them. My mother made it a point to tell me that she is having company, so I assumed it was male company. I'd give her some alone time while I went to grab a bite to eat. After I ironed everything, I jumped in the shower.

When I shut the shower off, I could hear voices. The second voice was very familiar, and belonged to someone that I didn't want to see. It was Lailani, laughing and talking to my mother like they were the best of friends. Lailani and my mother had built a bond while we were together, but I had no idea that they still conversed. I took my precious time drying my body off and getting dressed. Once I opened the door, I knew I would be forced to speak to her against my will.

Instead of going to the living room, I went straight back to the bedroom. I had to put my dirty clothes away, plus I was still not ready to see Lailani. They were both aware that I don't like surprises, and I felt like I had been set up. I was sure my mama invited her over on

8

purpose; that's why she wanted me to get up and get dressed. My mama was always doing something, whether good or bad, and that's why I tried to stay away from her. She was unpredictable, and now I was in the middle of one of her plots. If I just stayed in the room, maybe I wouldn't have to be a part of whatever she had planned.

I had just picked up my phone to call Jug when the bedroom door swung open. My mother stood there looking at me.

"What's up?" I asked.

"Someone wants to see you."

"Mama, why you…" but before I could finish my question, Lailani appeared in the doorway.

"Hey Saint," she spoke as she walked into the room. The first thing I noticed was the rock on her finger. Seeing that ring sent me through all type of emotions. I was a little hurt because she was engaged so soon. I felt confused on why she was here and she had a man; and third, I felt relieved that she had another man. Hopefully, she had let this thing between her and I go.

"'Sup Lani?"

"You look nice."

"Thanks, and so do you," I said nonchalantly.

"Can we talk?"

"Actually, I was about to go get a bite to eat."

"We're hungry," my mother interjected. I took a deep breath and looked over at her. "What? We are. Ain't you hungry, Lailani?"

"Yes," she answered, looking at my mother.

"Alright, whatever," I said, giving in. It would be easy to dismiss Lailani, but my mother was going to come regardless. She didn't take no for an answer, and especially not from me.

"Let me go get changed," my mother smiled and pulled the door closed as she walked away.

"How have you been?" Lailani asked.

"I'm okay, but not as good as you I see," I answered, looking at her ring.

She laughed. "I'm not engaged if that's what you're thinking. I wear this to keep the guys away."

"Is that right?"

"Yeah, you know I wouldn't go getting engaged to someone else this quick. I'm still in love with you, Saint."

"You need to get out, because there is no future for us."

She walked up on me, threw her arms around my neck, and kissed me. "Please don't say that, Saint," she kissed me again. "I know I fucked up, but I love you."

Her kisses were hypnotic. For a second, I forgot about everything that she had put me through. It was more seconds than that once she started rubbing her hand against my muscle. Slowly, I began to kiss her back. Once I did that, she began tugging at my pants.

"Lani…"

"Shh," she said, placing her finger over my lips. I looked at her while she pulled them down. She dropped down to her knees, sucking me up. *Damn.* I wanted her to stop, but at the same time I didn't. It'd been weeks since I burst a nut, and I wanted one. While she sucked my dick, I imagined she was Heaven. I missed her like shit, but I have been too stubborn to call. I'd picked up the phone several time to call, and my pride wouldn't let me dial. For the past few weeks I'd been having morning sickness, and I was beginning to believe that the baby was indeed mine. My mother asked me about kids when she started having dreams about fish. I thought it was just some old folks superstition shit until I start vomiting.

"Fuck," I whispered as I felt my nut approaching. She sucked faster until I exploded in her mouth. She swallowed it all, then looked up at me and smiled.

"Are y'all ready?" I heard my mother call out.

I wiped my dick off with the towel I had just dried off with, and pulled my pants up. As we walked out of the room, I slapped Lailani on her ass. She giggled and kept walking.

My mother wanted to go to Olive Garden, so that's where we ended up. She was going on and on about some wine that only they had; not to mention, she had a specific one that she wanted to go to. I wasn't into Italian food like that, but I'd eat the bullshit today. Like I said, there was no arguing with Sharon Mitchell.

Today, I set a new record for the fastest eater in America. I was ready to pay the tab and leave. My mother and Lailani were becoming obnoxious the more they sipped on that wine. The wine was running through my mother, so she was going back and forth to the bathroom the entire time. Her next bathroom break was going to be at the house, because I was ready to go.

While my mother was gone, I went ahead and paid for our meals. As soon as slid my card through the machine, Legend came to speak to me. I was caught off guard so I spoke to him, but I didn't know what to say to Heaven. I wanted to say something, but she snatched Legend away so fast and walked off before I had the chance. Without thinking about Lailani or my mother, I jumped up from the seat to chase her. Seeing her had me in my feelings all over again.

Running after Heaven was a bad idea. She met me with an attitude, and that ignorant *if* shit fell out of my mouth. I said the same dumb shit that I told myself I wouldn't say to her again. True, I had a pea sized amount of doubt that the baby was mine, but I swore I wouldn't say it to her face again. *Fuck.* I wanted to walk away and start over, then Lailani brought her ugly ass over to introduce herself. Lailani was far from ugly, but right now that was what she was being. She grabbed my hand and began to pull me away. Like a dummy, I was going until I realize what just happened.

"Let my fuckin' hand go," I said, snatching away from Lailani.

"Who was that, Saint?"

"None of your business," I replied as I watched Heaven and the boys get into the car.

"You fuckin' her?"

"What the fuck did I just say? You not my bitch, so stop asking me questions. Now where the fuck is my mama?"

"She's probably still inside."

I hit the unlock button on the keypad. "Get in the truck, I'm going to go get her."

She folded her arms and walked away. I jogged back toward the restaurant to find Sharon's drunk ass.

I pulled up in front of my mother's house and sat there. Lailani looked at me smiling, but I had a straight face. I looked in the backseat at my mother, and she opened the door to get out. Lailani was still sitting, so I looked back at her.

"What you waiting on?" I asked.

"What you mean what am I waiting on? You just gon' drop me off?"

"Yeah. What else did you think was going to happen?"

"Well I thought since I sucked yo' dick, we were going to spend tonight together."

"That's what you get for thoughtin', 'cause you thought wrong."

"Fuck you, Saint," she fumed, opening the door.

"Thanks for the head though, it was the shit."

She slammed the car door in my face and stomped off. I chuckled to myself, then drove off. This shit between Heaven and I have to be fixed, so that is what I was going to do. Seeing her made me think about all of the good times we shared on the drive home. I missed her and the boys, and I had to make things right. I was almost sure that was my kid that she was carrying, so I needed to go ahead and man up.

As I pulled into the condominium complex, I dialed Heaven's number. She didn't answer, so I hung up and called again. Since I hadn't been around, I didn't want to walk up and ring the doorbell. I had no idea what she had told the boys, and I didn't want to confuse them. It wasn't really my style of contact, but I sent her a text message.

Me: Can we talk?

Heaven: Talk to your fiancée."

Me: ????

Heaven: ….

Me: I'm outside. Please come out and talk to me Heaven. I think you got your wires crossed.

A minute went by without a response from her, then I saw her porch light come on. She opened the door, and I stepped out the truck. As we walked toward each other, I could tell that she was upset. She looked like she had been crying, and I wanted to know why.

"What's wrong, Heav?"

"You, Saint," her voice cracked. "How could you?"

"Heaven," I whispered as I pulled her close to me, and secured my arms around her. "I am so sorry. That shit today was some bullshit. My mama set me up by bringing Lailani over, we ended up going to dinner, and…just know that it's nothing at all going on between us. Look, I think we need to sit down and have an in-depth conversation. Everything was happening so fast between us before, without us really knowing each other. Neither of our exes want to see us together, and we're letting them ruin us. I let Flex get in my head, now here you are crying over a damn ring that I have nothing to do with. They're playing mind games with us, and I'm not down with that shit no more. If you want to try this again on some for real shit, I'm with it all the way. If not I understand, but know that I am going to be around for my child, and not no weekend dad type shit either. It's all up to you baby, so just let me know."

CHAPTER 3

Heaven

Saint was in the middle of my driveway professing his love for me, and my emotions were getting the best of me. As much as I wanted to be mad at him, I missed him too much. I did not know how much of what he was saying was true about things between him and Lailani, but I could smell her on him when he pulled me close. It almost made me gag.

"You smell like her," I said, pulling away from him.

"She hugged me."

"What else did she do?"

"Let's not talk about it," Saint said, pulling me close again but I pulled away.

"I can't do this right now. You of all people know what I put up with dealing with Flex, so you don't think I know when a man has kissed a woman or has been intimate with her? Nigga, it's lipstick on your collar. You smell like her. I bet anything it's a ring of lipstick around your dick because she's a messy ass bitch. I peeped that shit in the restaurant."

I was pissed at myself for going off the way that I did. We were not together, so he was free to stick his dick wherever he pleased. I could not keep the tears from falling. Saint was right; we moved at light speed. We were two hurt people trying to get away from our past, and we fell into each other's arms; but it was doomed to begin with.

"Don't be like that, Heav. The last thing I wanted to do was make you cry," Saint said, trying to pull me close again.

"Don't," I held my hands up. "I can't stomach her smell."

"What can I do to make things right?"

"I need time, Saint. You really hurt me. I don't think I can go back to things just being all shiny and new."

"I understand," Saint answered.

We stood in silence for a few moments. I did not know what to say. I wanted to be with him, but I could not shake all the things he had said to me. I could tell that he still did not believe that our baby was his, and that was problem number one. I could not be with a man who did not think that I was loyal to him.

"I need to go inside," I said, finally breaking the silence.

"Can I come in?"

"I don't want the boys to get the wrong impression."

"Tell me what I can do, Heaven. I don't think I can go too much longer without you."

"I just need time, Saint. I'm taking a leave of absence from my job once school is out in a couple of weeks, and going to visit my parents in South Carolina."

"So you're running away?"

"No, but there I can clear my head. I don't have to do the back and forth."

"I need you, Heav," Saint said again, this time placing his hand on my belly. "I don't want my baby growing up without two parents in the house together."

"Saint…just let me think about it," I said again before turning to go in the house.

I could not bear to be out there any longer because I did not want to be the fool and take him back so easily. If Saint wanted me, he was going to have to work for me. I watched Saint from my window for a few minutes. I wanted to open my door and let him back in because I had not had sex in weeks, but he smelled like her. Maybe another day. My phone vibrated in my pocket. I pulled it out and saw that I had a text.

SAINT: I'm not gonna stop chasing you.

HEAVEN: I need time.

SAINT: You got it. I love you.

HEAVEN: I love you too.

I heard Saint's truck crank up as I sat down on the sofa. I had been on the phone with Tressa before he came over. She wanted to know all the details about what went down in the parking lot at the restaurant. She sympathized with me and let me cry it out. I would have never gotten that kind of support from Kalina. She would have had a field day with telling me how all niggas are just alike, and I needed to use them before they used me.

Since it was too late to call Tressa back, I decided to scroll through Facebook before I went to bed. I still had not unfriended Kalina, so she was heavy on my timeline posting pictures of her mystery man. If I were her, I would have been given up. That nigga did not want to be seen with her. She was always posting pictures of them holding hands or of his hat-covered face. She was starting to look super thirsty, and that was not a good look. I wanted to reach out to her and say something, but I did not want her to think I was hating or anything. I did want to know who dude was though. I wished that I knew more people so I could get the tea.

Ж

BANG! BANG! BANG!

I was startled out of my sleep by someone banging on my door. I hated when that shit happened. I checked the clock and it was eleven in the morning. The boys had not even tried to wake me up, but I could hear them in the kitchen talking. I loved to eavesdrop on their conversations because they were so funny, but I had to see who was at my door first. I opened the door to a delivery man.

"Heaven Santana?" he asked.

"Yes, that's me."

"Sign here please." He handed me an electronic notepad and I signed my signature as best as I could. "It's quite a big order, so if you'll bear with me for one moment..."

I watched as he turned back to his truck and pulled out two large vases filled to the brim with Calla Lilies. My heart melted at the sight. Saint knew that I loved those flowers. The delivery man brought them to my door and I started to close it.

"No ma'am, I have a couple more items," he said, stopping me.

I was awestruck. I did not know what he had, but I wanted to find out. I watched him as he pulled out a huge Edible Arrangements basket and a gift bag.

"You can sit it on the coffee table," I instructed.

"Okay…well that's it. Have a nice day."

I smiled politely as he walked back to his truck. I closed the door and went straight for the gift bag, and pulled out the card:

I won't stop fighting for you. - Saint.

There were several jewelry boxes in it. I opened the first long box and was blown away. He had sent me a diamond bracelet. The other boxes contained matching earrings and a matching necklace. I smiled on the inside because no man had ever done something so nice. Although I was not ready to jump right back into things with Saint, I still owed him a thank you for trying.

HEAVEN: *Thank you for the flower and the jewelry, they're beautiful.*

SAINT: *You're beautiful. I meant what I said.*

HEAVEN: *Okay.*

SAINT: *Eat the fruit and stop feeding my baby junk.*

I smiled at his last text. Saint really knew how to get under my skin and into my heart. I knew that with all the effort he was putting in, it was going to be hard to stay mad at him. We just needed to get our exes in check because they would surely be our downfall.

CHAPTER 4

Saint

After leaving Heaven's place the other night, I didn't bother going back to my mother's house. Instead, I went where I should have gone in the first place—my grandmother's house. She raised me, and she knew how to talk to me. The only reason that I didn't want to go before was because I was upset. She knew me well, and she would have known something was wrong. I didn't want to talk to her about everything that was going on at the moment. She was going to try to give me her advice, and I wanted to think for myself. I couldn't keep running to her every time I have a little problem.

This morning was no different than the other mornings. I woke up and had to rush to the bathroom to vomit. Last night I made sure not to eat anything, but I still had to regurgitate. When I emerged from the bathroom, my grandmother was sitting in the living room. She had a big cup of coffee that she was sipping while she watched the morning news.

"Morning, Maw Maw."

"Hey Paw" My grandmother always called me Paw or Paw Paw. I

23

was named after her grandfather, so she called me what she called him. "You ready for some breakfast?"

"Nah, I'll just get me a cup of coffee also."

"Are you sick, baby?"

"Something like that."

She smiled at me while she sat her cup on the coaster. "So you're the fish?"

"What?"

"You're the fish that we have been dreaming about. Did you get that damn Lailani girl pregnant, Paw?"

"Hell nah."

"Well did you get someone else pregnant?"

"I think so."

"What you mean, you think so? Either you did or you didn't, and from the past few mornings you've had, I will guess you did."

"I know, but..."

"Sit down, Paw Paw." I walked over and grabbed the seat next to her. She patted my knee then turned to face me. "Paw, you know I don't get into your personal business. But if you have a child on the way, you need to acknowledge it."

"I am, but it's hard because I'm not exactly sure. She was dealing with her other children's father, and he mentioned that it is his baby."

"Paw, look at me. I've watched you eat, sleep, and vomit all day— that is your child. You need to stand up and be a man."

"You know I'm going to do that, no doubt; it was just a lot going on between us."

"Well I'm gon' tell you like my mama told me, a man that doesn't take care of his children will forever have bad luck. Anything that you try to accomplish will crumb and fail. You see what happened to your father. You've got out of prison and made something of yourself; don't lose it all with that constipated thinking. Sharon has had dreams of fish and so have I, so I believe it's yours."

I was sitting there lost for words. Everything that she was telling me was the absolute truth. The more I thought about Heaven and me, the more I realized that it was impossible for the baby to be Flex's. He hadn't been around like that, and we were pretty much always together. I fucked up big time with Heaven. She was giving me the cold shoulder now, but I wasn't done trying to get her back. Whatever it takes for us to be together I am willing to do, no matter how long it takes.

The talk with my grandmother actually did some good. She helped screw my head back on straight, so now I was thinking with a clear mind. My grandmother had embroidered in my brain that the baby was mine. I didn't know if it was some old folk superstition shit or what, but I believed her. If I didn't trust what anyone in the world said, I trusted my grandmother's words. She was the smartest and wisest person I knew.

I had to go back to the drawing board and start all the way over. Being with Heaven and the kids was important to me, so I had to do things right this time around. We had to become friends first in order for me to fully trust her. I wanted to start over and date her. Twenty years from now, I wanted to be able to tell our child a beautiful story about us. The story that had been written so far was not the one I want to tell.

Since I hired a new crew, I didn't have to go out to the job sites as much. I usually went out for the consultation and the final showing. There was plenty of work for me to do at the office, so I stopped there first. Business was booming, and I had to stay on top of that. Once the winter came the work stopped, so I had to make sure my crew had every job possible.

While I worked, I couldn't get Heaven off my brain. I got online and began to order a few gifts. Buying her gifts wasn't going to get her back, but I was hoping by Friday she would accept my invitation for a date. Every day this week, a different number of gifts would be delivered, and a dress and heels were to arrive on Friday. I wanted to treat her to a romantic date just to make her happy again. Sex wasn't on my mind as much as getting her back. I'd tell her that we could remove that part for now, and spend time getting to know each other.

After returning all the messages and setting up consultations, I packed up to leave. My work for the day was done, now I had to go meet up with the realtor. I was looking for another house to move into. I cursed myself for giving up my spot to move in with Heaven. It left me homeless, and I would never do that shit again. Even if we decided to get back together, I would keep my house this time. I'd be damned if I got put out of anything else and didn't have a place to go.

My last house was pretty basic, but my next one would be anything but that. The next house has to be at least four bedrooms, and I wanted a pool in the backyard. I wanted a lot of space and yard to maneuver around. I requested to look at homes in the new neighborhood not too far from my grandmother. She was getting older, and I wanted to be close to her. Work had consumed most of my time, so I hadn't spent that much time with her.

When I pulled up in front of the possible house, the realtor Michelle was already standing out front. Michelle was Manny's wife, and he recommended her to me. They had a nice home, so I had faith that she would find the perfect one for me.

"How you doing, Michelle?" I spoke as I stepped out the truck.

"I'm blessed Saint, how are you?"

"Beyond blessed."

"Alright then. Well, let's go inside so I can show you around."

I held my hand out for her to take the lead.

As I stepped into the home, I knew this was the one. It gave me a vibe like none of the others gave off. It had way more space on the inside than I envisioned. This house had five bedrooms, which included two master suites. I wanted to get something of this nature in case my grandmother ended up needing assistance.

When I walked into the third bedroom, the baby's nursery came to mind. The entire room screamed it to me. It had a connecting door to the master bedroom, so it was perfect. If Heaven and I didn't work out, I needed my baby in a room close to me. I couldn't decorate for shit, so I decided to give Heaven the job of decorating the nursery however she wanted it.

"So what do you think?" Michelle asked, startling me.

"I think it's perfect."

"Do you want to go ahead and put a bid in for it?"

I looked around and smiled. "Yes, I would."

"Great. I'll go make the call now. Take your time to look around some more if you like."

"Thanks Michelle."

"No problem."

She smiled, then walked out of the room. This house was right at three hundred thousand, so she was going to get a fat commission check from this. She was definitely deserving of it, because she found just what I wanted. Not only that, Manny told me that her sales had been down and they were falling behind on bills. I couldn't give him another raise, but her commission should help them out.

Once I left from seeing the house, I stopped by my mother's house. All of my things were still over there, and I was tired of buying things to wear every day. I wasn't ready to face her because she was trying to talk to me about Lailani. For some reason, she liked her and wanted us to be together. Even after the stories I had told her, she still wanted us to try again. I'd never taken my mother's advice, so I wasn't going to start now. She didn't know how to decipher what was good for me, and what wasn't. Hell, she didn't even know what was good or bad for herself.

I was packing up the last of my things when my mother walked into the room. She walked over and sat on the side of the bed.

"So you're gone, huh?" she asked.

"Yep, I'm out of your hair."

"I didn't mind you being here."

"I know, but I'd rather stay with Maw Maw."

"So is it true? Do you have a baby on the way?"

"Maw Maw told you?"

"Of course she did. So?"

"Yes."

"Well, who is this mystery lady?"

"Her name is Heaven."

"Why are you keeping her a secret?"

"That wasn't the plan, but things moved fast then went left before I was able to."

"So you're not together?"

"No, not at the moment. And mama, don't go tellin' Lailani my business."

"I have to tell her something. She loves you Saint, and she was thinking that you were getting back together."

"I don't know why she would think that, I told her that there was no way that we would get back together."

"Saint, you leave me in a tough position."

"No I'm not, because it's not your business. Stay out of my business, and stop talking to Lailani. I don't owe her shit and neither do you. Stop talking to her."

"You are not my father Saint, remember that."

"Well whatever. That's exactly why I'm going to stay with Maw Maw. You seem to have everyone's back but mine, and I can't deal with this shit. I got too much to deal with already to add your drama to the list. I'm gon' put it to you like this—dead that shit with her, or leave me alone."

"Saint?"

"I mean it, Ma. I'm trying to work on things with Heaven, and I don't need Lailani hanging around. Her being around will cause a big problem."

"Is this Heaven chick insecure or something?"

"It's not about her insecurities, it's about Lailani trying to pretend that we are something that we aren't."

"Okay," she said, exhaling deeply. "But I still have to tell Lailani something when she calls."

I stood up from the floor and grabbed my bag. "Tell her to go to hell, Ma. Tell her to go straight to hell."

I turned to walk out the room before she had a chance to reply. She had some thinking to do, and I wanted to leave her to it. If she wanted to talk to Lailani, that was cool with me; but I wouldn't be talking to her. She hadn't been a big part of my life, so I wasn't going to miss her much.

CHAPTER 5

Heaven

$\mathcal{S}$aint had been showering me with gifts all week. I had to admit, I loved the special treatment, but Saint could not buy my forgiveness. By the time Friday had come, I received a package with a dress and a pair of shoes. The dress was a white floral print sundress with an empire waist that hid my baby bump well. The fabric was flowy so it was very breathable, and it was comfortable because the Texas heat was not agreeing with my pregnancy. Saint had picked out a pair of flat sandals that laced up my legs. I felt cute once I pulled my hair into a high bun and left my bangs out. I sent Saint a text thanking him for the outfit.

HEAVEN: Thank you for the dress and shoes. They are nice.

SAINT: I was hoping you would wear it out on a date with me tonight.

HEAVEN: I'll have to ask Tressa or Vedra if they will watch the boys.

SAINT: Who are they?

HEAVEN: Some new friends I met.

SAINT: Are they anything like your girl?

HEAVEN: No and don't be like that. Kalina has her own special set of problems.

SAINT: Yeah. That bitch need to be committed.

HEAVEN: Are we gonna talk about her the whole time?

My phone vibrated in my hand, indicating I had a call. Saint was calling me. It was so much easier to text him. The words flowed from my fingertips quicker than they escaped my lips.

"Hello?" I answered.

"We don't have to talk about her anymore. But is you gonna let a nigga take you out or what, Heav? I miss the fuck out of you."

My panties moistened at the sound of his voice. This pregnancy had me super horny, and I knew that being in the same room with Saint probably would end up with me on his dick at some point.

"Let me make some calls and get a sitter," I finally said.

"Cool."

"Saint?"

"Yeah?"

"It's just dinner. That's it. I'm still not ready to go there with you again."

"I understand, and that's all I ask for is dinner."

"Okay," I smiled. "I'll make some calls and let you know what I come up with."

"I love you, Heaven."

"I love you too."

I hung up the phone on cloud nine. I called Vedra first to see if she could watch the boys. Tressa was bound to have a football game she had to be at since it was Friday night. Vedra agreed to watch the boys for me. She and Catana were going to the movies, so I offered to pay for the movies and popcorn. Vedra happily agreed and I told her that I would drop the kids off in a couple of hours. I texted Saint as soon as I got off the phone.

HEAVEN: Vedra is going to watch them. She's taking them to the movies. So you need to pay for 4 tickets. I'll buy the snacks.

Shit, I wanted him to pay for it all because he owed me that much for believing Flex's punk ass to start with, but I was gonna let him breathe on this one.

SAINT: I'll buy the snacks too. What time does it start?

HEAVEN: 8.

SAINT: I'll pick ya'll up by 6:30.

HEAVEN: OK. TTYL.

I smiled because I was genuinely excited about spending time with Saint. I really did miss him. I just did not want to fall back into our old routine. I did, however, want to floss in the new diamonds Saint had bought me. I went to my jewelry box and put on the necklace, bracelet, and earrings. I checked myself out in the mirror and loved what I saw. Even with my pregnant belly, my bae had me looking good. He just could not know he was my bae again. I wanted to see him beg some more. I got the kids dressed and let them know that Vedra was taking them to the movies while Saint and I went to dinner to talk about some things. They were excited to see *The Jungle Book.*

Saint showed up at six on the dot. He rang the doorbell and greeted me with flowers. I was blushing like a school girl. The boys were super excited to see him. They jumped into his arms as soon as he walked through the door. I had to excuse myself to the restroom to wipe some tears from my eyes and fix my make-up. The ride to Vedra's house was loud. Saint and the boys talked non-stop about everything from the playoffs and how they thought that Steph Curry and Golden State would take the championship, to the upcoming football season. I sat quietly and just listened to the sound of old times.

Once we dropped off the boys, the car fell to an awkward silence. I did not know what to talk about. I watched Saint drum the steering wheel of his 2016 Chevy Suburban. I wanted to ask what happened to his truck, but I did not want to make any assumptions. The car was nice and roomy, as if he were planning for a family. I smiled because maybe he did think that there was a chance for us to survive.

"So…ummmm, I see you got you a new ride," I said nonchalantly.

"Yeah. I had to make room for the baby," he smirked, looking over at me. I looked out the window.

"What happened to your truck?"

"I still have it. I'm just using it for work."

"Oh," I said quietly. "Well this is nice."

"Thanks. What do you want to eat?"

"I thought you made a plan."

"I remembered that you change your mind a lot these days, so I wanted to give you a choice."

"I want a steak," I said.

"You need to chill with that red meat. It's not good for my baby," Saint shot back.

"*Your* baby?" I asked with a raised eyebrow. "Weren't we at *if* the other day?"

"I was being an ass," Saint said.

I smiled because he admitted to being an ass. I sat back in the soft leather seat and watched as Saint gave in and turned into Pappas Bros. Steakhouse parking lot.

"I'll eat a salad to make you happy," I smiled as he parked the car.

"You better eat the whole damn head of lettuce," he said, getting out of the car. He opened my door for me and held my hand all the way to the door of the restaurant.

Dinner was amazing. I had a salad and extra broccoli to make up for the huge ribeye I ordered. Saint mean mugged me as I ate every bit. My appetite was always on ten with this baby. I ate a hell of a lot more with this pregnancy than I had with either of the boys. I thought Saint was about to lose his shit when I ordered the Chocolate Midnight Cake for dessert and the cheesecake to go.

"Yo' ass gon' be as big as a house," he shot.

"I walk it off. I'm just enjoying being pregnant."

Saint sat back and sipped his Hennessey as I dug into my cake.

"It's sooooo good," I laughed, waving a fork full of cake in his face. "You want some."

"I want you."

The smile faded from my face. I had spent the night avoiding the conversation because we had some serious issues to work through.

"It's just dinner, Saint," I said shakily.

"Heaven, it's more than that and you know it. I thought I wanted to take things slow because we jumped so fast into things, but I am having a hard time without you. I talked to my grandmother and she spit some real shit to me. I have to have you and the boys in my life."

I sat back and wiped the tears from my eyes. Saint knew what the fuck he was doing playing on my emotions. He knew I was pregnant and emotional. Why did that nigga have to be so fucking fine and romantic? He knew the exact way back into my good graces, but I had to stay strong; he needed to work a little harder. I did not want to answer him right away, so I just smiled at him and scanned the dining room. I thought I had seen Kalina sitting at a table across the room, but I knew that it could not be her.

"Saint...let me think about it. As much as I love you and I love you sooo much, you hurt me by thinking I wasn't anything but loyal to you," I stared Saint in his eyes, but the man sitting across the room caught my eye. "I got to go to the bathroom."

Saint stood and helped me stand up. I walked with a purpose across the dining room floor. My eyes had to be playing tricks on me. The bathroom was not in their direct view so I would be able to make sure I was not imagining things, and I damn sure was not. I knew I had seen Kalina when we sat down, but what I was not expecting was for that trifling ass bitch to be having dinner with Flex's stupid ass. I turned around and marched directly back to our table.

"Let's go," I said, grabbing my purse.

"What's wrong?" Saint asked, pulling out his wallet and putting two one-hundred-dollar bills on the table.

"I found out who Kalina's new man is," I hissed as I grabbed his hand and we walked out of the door.

"Who?"

"Flex."

CHAPTER 6

Saint

*H*eaven pulled me out of the restaurant so fast that I didn't even see Flex or Kalina's face. She was hightailing it back the car, stomping like Sophia on *The Color Purple*, pulling me like a child. I knew she was upset about seeing her best friend with her baby daddy, but I didn't see why we had to cut our night short. I was actually happy that the both of them were together. That would keep them out of our hair. The mood was definitely killed for the night, and we still hadn't resolved much.

The night was still young, and I was not ready for it to end. I wasn't going to let Flex or Kalina mess things up for us. My focus was on Heaven and the relationship that we were trying to build. I don't give one, two, or three fucks about neither one of them at all. Kalina wasn't supposed to be a topic of our conversation tonight, so I had to redirect things quickly. We jumped back in the truck and headed to downtown Dallas.

After parking in the West End parking lot, we walked down to the strip. There were horse and carriage rides down there, and I wanted to take Heaven on one. That would give us plenty of alone time to talk about whatever. She had been quiet since we left the restaurant, so I knew she is in her feelings. As far as I could see everything made her emotional, but I didn't want those two occupying her mind.

We walked hand in hand up the street, not saying a word. As we approached the horses, Heaven looked over at me and smiled. That smile was so damn hypnotizing to me. I wanted more than anything to keep it there.

"You ready to take a ride?" I asked.

"Of course."

"Excuse me sir," I said, walking up on the driver. "Can we get a ride?"

"Yes sir," he replied, jumping from the front of the carriage.

I helped Heaven climb into the carriage, then jumped in behind her. She looked at me once I sat down, but this time her face was scrunched up.

"What's wrong?"

"Maybe this wasn't such a good idea. All I smell is horse ass."

I laughed, then pulled her close to me. "Just smell on me, baby."

"That might work a little."

I secured my arms around her, then the driver pulled off.

Dallas had the best skyline ever, and I'm not just saying that because this is my hometown. For the past few years, the city had done a lot of building and upgrading. It was a sight to see at night, but it was just the beginning. In ten years it would look like a new city, because it looks way different from 10 years ago. When I got out of prison a few years back, I was confused as hell trying to drive.

Heaven was still quiet, and I didn't like it. I knew Flex and Kalina fucked her mood up, but I was trying to rearrange that. We had too many other things to worry about besides them.

"Tell me what's eating your brain," I said, starting the conversation.

"A lot."

"Like what?"

"Flex and Kalina betraying me."

"I thought we weren't going to think or talk about them? This date is supposed to be about us, and what we have going on. What they're doing is fucked up, but this is about us Heav."

"I know, it's just bothered me."

"Well don't think about it. I don't want you stressed out while you're carrying our child."

"You stress me too, Saint."

"I'm not trying to," I said, rubbing her belly. "I'm trying to build a life with you that's stress-free for the both of us. I know I acted out, but I was hurt. You just don't understand all the emotions I went through when he said the baby was his. All I could think about were the times that I've seen him up on you. You're not looking at your relationship with him through my eyes. I know I should have had more trust in you, but I have to believe my eyes too. You know what I'm saying? Just like when you thought I was engaged to Lailani 'cause she had a ring on. If I need to apologize again for how I was treating you, I will. I'm so sorry for inflicting unnecessary pain on you. I know these are just words, but I am willing to show you how sorry I am. I've wanted you since the first day I saw you, Heaven Santana, and I won't stop trying to get you."

She was tearing up like she always did. Her hormones were all out of control, so she cried when she was happy and sad. It confused me because I couldn't decipher between the two sometimes. I used my thumb to wipe the tears away before they began to slide down her beautiful face.

"I'm sorry too, Saint. I didn't mean to hurt you either."

"I know. I'm not holding it against you because I was hella wrong."

I kissed her on her forehead, then we went back to being silent. We hadn't resolved everything, but we were on the right track. I'm not sure if we were going to get back together or not though. If nothing else, I wanted us to be friends.

Our semi-romantic date was now over. I pulled into Heaven's driveway and stopped. Several thoughts went through my head as we looked into each other's eyes. I still wasn't ready for the night to end. She wanted some space, and I was going to respect that.

"I enjoyed my time with you this evening, Heaven."

"So did I."

"I talked to my mama and grandmother about us, and they want to meet the woman that's carrying their grandchild."

"Oh, okay," she replied slowly.

"Are you scared?"

"Not at all. When do they want to meet?"

"Whenever you want to. Just let me know and I'll set it up."

I knew I wasn't going inside, but I walked Heaven to the door. She unlocked the door then turned to face me. I grabbed her by her waist and pulled her close to me. She wrapped her arms around my neck, then we went at it kissing. My hands drifted down to her butt to cop a feel. The pregnancy was putting some fat on her ass. I couldn't help but to squeeze it one time while my hands were down there.

Heaven had those bedroom eyes when I pulled away. The kiss was erotic and it had both of us hot. I had to pull away to avoid going any further.

"I'm going to call you in the morning."

"Okay," she said exhaling.

"Have a good night, alright?"

"Alright," she smiled.

I kissed her once more on her neck, then turned to walk away. My dick was beginning to grow, so I had to get far away from her. I hustled back to my truck and jumped inside. I watched as she opened the door and disappeared inside. My mind and body told me to go back and knock on that door. She was in control of the situation, so I had to let her be. I turned the engine over and backed out of the driveway.

Instead of going to my grandmother's house, I drove to the bar. If I went home, all I would do was think about Heaven. I didn't want to spend the next few hours horny and alone. A few drinks would put me just where I needed to be. Once I get a good buzz going, I would be able to sleep well.

Since I was on the north side of town, I drove to Austin Avenue. They played good music, but they also had a bar and pool tables. When I walked inside, some girls were on the stage doing karaoke. One sounded alright, but the other one was horrible. It was all drunken fun, so everyone was going along with it.

I walked past the crowd through the doors that led to the bar. They were playing rap music in this room. It was a completely different feel from the room I just exited. Weed smoke filled the air, and the crowd was more hood. I walked up to the bar where the bartender was standing.

"What can I get you?" she smiled.

"Hennessey on the rocks."

"Coming right up."

She turned to grab the bottle, and I was faced with a big fake ass. She was a pretty girl, so I don't know why she would do that to herself. It would be different if it looked natural, but it wasn't proportioned right. Her thighs were skinny and her ass was colossal.

"7.50," she said, sitting the cup in front of me. I pulled my credit card out and handed it to her. "Do you want to start a tab?"

"Sure, why not."

It was a little after midnight, so I'd stick around for an hour so. The crowd and the music was live, and I wanted to enjoy it. After being stuck in the house for the past few weeks, I needed to get out. I wish Heaven was here, but again I wouldn't want her in this crowd.

I was halfway through my drink when I saw Lailani walking

toward me smiling. What the hell was she doing here? She didn't even stay or hang out on this side of town. I was looking forward to enjoying myself tonight, but it looked like I might have to cut it short.

"Hey baby," she spoke.

This girl just doesn't quit. "I'm not your baby."

"Not right now."

"Lailani, what do you want?"

"You know what I want," she said, grabbing my package.

I brushed her hand out of the way and stepped back. "Don't do that. Don't disrespect me like that."

"Disrespect you?" she laughed. "How am I disrespecting you?"

"You're putting your hands on me, and I don't want you to."

"Oh, you don't want me to?" she asked, stepping forward.

"No. I told you that there is nothing between us, we're not getting back together."

"That's not what you were saying the other day when my lips were around your dick."

She placed her hand on my chest, and I jerked it away.

"I'm not fuckin' playing with yo' ass. Stop with these childish ass games."

"How am I childish for wanting my man back?"

"You're not getting me. I'm getting ready to have a baby, and I'm with my child's mother. Understand that you and I are over. Don't go calling or visiting my mama or none of that shit. When you see me out, don't say shit to me."

"You got a baby on the way?"

"Yeah I do."

"How could you do that to me, Saint?"

"I ain't do shit to you, you did everything to me."

"You know I wanted children with you. I begged you for them, and you said you didn't want any."

"I didn't want any with you, Lailani. You think I want the mother of my children to be a hoe? Hell nah, I don't want my daughter to have a stripper for a mother."

"That's fucked up, Saint."

"What was fucked up was you fuckin' a nigga my bed, Lailani. That right there ended us forever. I don't trust you and I never will."

"I'm sorry for that, Saint."

"Keep ya sorry. And please leave me alone, you fuckin' with my buzz right now."

"You're always being an ass."

"And you're always giving up the ass. Get the fuck away from me before I get mad."

"Fuck you, Saint," she said, walking off.

"Yeah, you want to don't you?"

As she walked away, she held up her middle finger. I laughed to myself, then turned to face the bar. It was time to close out my tab and go to the house. I need to go to sleep and start all the way over. When I woke up, I thought today was going to be a good day, but Flex, Kalina, and now Lailani had ruined it.

CHAPTER 7

Heaven

Last night, I could feel Saint's manhood pressing against me. I wanted to invite him in, but I knew that would be doing the opposite of making him earn my forgiveness. I went to bed horny instead, with Flex and Kalina on my mind. I should not have been surprised because they both were scandalous. I wanted to call and curse both of them out, but I did not want to look crazy to them. I slept horribly.

"You look like shit," Vedra said, looking at me over the top of her sunglasses. She was dropping the kids off for me.

"I feel like shit."

"What happened to you? I thought you and Saint would have been making up all night long."

"Tressa is on her way over. I'm gonna make breakfast for everyone. I got tea to spill," I said before walking into the kitchen.

Vedra followed me while the kids ran upstairs to play. She begged me to tell her what I had to tell them before Tressa showed up, but I told her it would be better if I did not have to repeat it. She finally relented as I pulled out the pots and pans I needed to make breakfast. My appetite was huge, so I planned on putting on a spread. I was making cheese grits, bacon, chicken tenders, Belgian waffles, hash browns, eggs, and biscuits. I pulled out the ingredients to make virgin mimosas. I couldn't have alcohol, but I definitely needed some.

"Damn, are you cooking for a small army?" Tressa asked, entering the kitchen.

"Between us and all our kids...yeah," I answered, stirring my grits and adding the cheese.

"It only looks like enough for you," she said, peeking into the pots.

"Shut up," I laughed, pushing her out of the way.

"Tressa is here now, so spill the tea," Vedra demanded.

I put the top back on the pot and turned the stove down before I faced them. I felt a lump form in my throat. I tried to pass Flex and Kalina being together off as no big deal to me, but that shit was eating me up. Kalina really proved that she was not a real friend to me. I did not know why I thought I needed confirmation.

"Spill it, Heaven," Tressa pushed, pouring herself a glass of orange juice.

"Flex and Kalina are together now."

Vedra and Tressa looked at me in a stunned silence.

"Get the fuck outta here!" Vedra yelled. "How did you find that out?"

"I saw them at the restaurant last night. Dallas is too fucking small for it to be so big."

"So… how are you feeling?" Tressa asked carefully.

I do not know why, but the tears started to fall. Tressa grabbed a paper towel and rushed to my side. I blew my nose with it. This was not supposed to be affecting me like this because I was supposed to be working on my relationship with Saint. I just could not help feeling betrayed. Vedra and Tressa watched me cry in silence for a few minutes before Vedra got up and left the kitchen. I figured she could not watch me cry any longer, so I pulled myself together as best as I could and focused my attention on the food. I still needed to cook the eggs and waffles, so I started to make the batter while Tressa watched me in silence. I had just pulled the biscuits out of the oven when Vedra came back into the kitchen followed by Saint. I almost dropped the damn pan.

"What are you doing here?" I asked him, hoping that my eyes were not puffy.

"I called him," Vedra said, taking a seat by Tressa. "I took your phone and called him."

Saint did not say anything. He just pulled me in for a hug. I felt like such a fool crying over Flex and Kalina when I had a man that treated me way better than Flex ever had.

"Let's talk," Saint said, taking me by the hand.

"Vee…can ya'll cook the bacon and eggs? The chicken will beep when it's ready to come out of the oven."

Vedra nodded her head as I followed Saint up to my bedroom. My heart was pounding as I closed the door behind us. I did not want him to think that I was stuck on Flex. Saint sat on my bed and patted the spot beside him for me to sit. I walked over slowly and sat next to him.

"Tell me what's the problem, Heav."

"I just want to hit them with my car," I said as my bottom lip quivered.

"So you want to have my baby in prison? That's what would happen if you did that," Saint laughed, wiping a tear from my eye. "Why does it bother you so much?"

"She was supposed to be my friend."

"Baby, you're a smart woman, so I know you are not that naïve to believe that a bitch like that was ever your friend. These hoes ain't loyal. You said it yourself…that bitch loved to see you miserable."

"I know," I whined, "but…"

"But my ass. Fuck her and fuck him. Fuck you worried about them bums when you got a nigga like me?"

"I'm being stupid."

"Nah… it's just the baby fucking with your brain," he smiled as he put his arm around my shoulder.

I laid my head on his shoulder. Saint wiped another tear from my eye before lifting my chin and placing his lips on mine. I missed his kiss. His lips tasted so good against mine. The same feelings I had from the previous night came rushing back to me. I pulled away from his kiss and stared into his eyes. I stood, pushing him back on the bed. I straddled his lap and kissed him deeply. Feeling his hands on my waist set me on fire. I sucked on his bottom lip as he palmed my breasts.

"Don't be using me to get your mind off yo' baby daddy," Saint said, pushing me up from our kiss.

"You're my baby daddy," I smiled wickedly.

I did not need Saint talking, so I kissed him again. I had not had sex in weeks, and my fingers no longer did the job. I was ready to stop taking it slow and hit the gas. That's just what I did. I used my hand to rub on Saint's hardening member. *Damn, I missed that shit.* Feeling it grow in my hand only soaked my panties more. I knew that there was a house full of people, but I needed to release the tension that I had built up.

"You sure you want to do this?" Saint asked as I moved to undo his pants.

"Please..." I begged, looking him dead in the eyes.

I guess I said the magic words, because Saint released his monster for me. I bit my bottom lip because I missed that pretty motherfucker. All I could think about was feeling him inside of me as I mounted him. I had to take it easy because I did not want to make too much noise. I rode him slow as he held onto my hips. I missed my man, and this shit felt so good and so right. I closed my eyes and threw my head back as he thrust his hips up into me.

"Shit," I let out softly.

"Ride this shit," he said as he grabbed the back of my neck and pulled me in for a kiss.

Saint thrust up into me, hitting my g-spot right on target. I wanted to scream out, but I bit down on his shoulder instead as I exploded all over him.

"I love you so much," I broke down into tears.

"I love you too, so can you forget about that fuck boy now?"

"It's not about that. I'm just hurt."

"Well put on your big girl panties and fuck them."

"I'd rather fuck you," I said, kissing him again.

"I know. Daddy got that good dick," he smiled, showing his beautiful teeth.

"Yes he do," I kissed him back before finally pulling him out of me and lying beside him.

"When's your next doctor's appointment, Heav?"

"Next week…I find out what we're having."

"Well, I want to be there," he said, rubbing his finger on my cheek.

I nodded my head in agreement. I was going to ask him to come anyway. It was time that we got ourselves on track. I needed to forget about Flex and Kalina before that shit tore us apart again.

CHAPTER 8

Saint

It was that day that I was introducing Heaven to my mother and grandmother. She said that she wasn't nervous about meeting them, but I was for her. I wasn't nervous about her meeting my grandmother, but my mother was wishy washy. She would play it cool then throw shade in the same breath. The fact that she was team Lailani had me not wanting to introduce them at all. My grandmother was always cool' I just prayed that Sharon was on her best behavior today.

Heaven was in her room getting dressed while I sat on the sofa channel surfing. She always took a long time to get dressed, so I knew I had time to watch an episode of something. A marathon of *Martin* was on, so I stopped there and tuned in. It was the episode when Varnell Hill came on, and that was my favorite one. I laughed as I watched Martin try not to laugh while Tommy Davidson explained what he had on his acres.

As the episode went off, I could hear Heaven coming down the stairs. I stood up and turned around anticipating her arrival. She sashayed around the corner looking spectacular. Her hair was all pinned up exposing her beautifully plump face. She was looking just like a glowing angel.

"Baby, you look good," I complimented her.

"Thank you."

"Turn around so I can see you," I held her hand while she twirled around. "Damn."

She laughed. "You sure know how to make a woman feel like a queen."

"You are a queen, know that shit." I pulled her in close to me and gave her a bear hug. She looked up at me, then we went in for a peck. I did not want to mess up the shine she had going on her lips. "You ready to go?"

"Yes, let me get my phone."

My grandmother was cooking dinner, so I pulled up in front of her house. I could see that my mother was already here. This dinner could go either way, but I'm praying for a civil one. If my mother had some drinks in her, she may not be and if she has talked to Lailani, she just might throw some shade. One thing that I did know was that my grandmother would have my back.

When I pushed the door open, the smell of Jiffy cornbread invaded my nostrils. Right then, my stomach began to growl. My grandmother could cook her ass off, and I could not wait to taste it all. We walked into the living room; my mother was sitting on the sofa watching television. When she laid eyes on us, she smiled and stood up.

"Mama, this is Heaven. Heaven this is my mother Sharon."

"Nice to meet you," Heaven spoke, extending her arm out.

"You too, Heaven. You look so pretty."

"Thank you."

"Nice job, Saint," she complimented me.

"Thanks. Come on Heav, let me go introduce you to Maw Maw."

Just as we were turning to walk away, Maw Maw came walking toward us. She had the brightest smile on her face as she dried her hands on a napkin.

"Maw Maw, this is Heaven."

"Of course she is. How are you doing, honey?" she beamed.

"I'm doing well."

"Well that's good. Take care of yourself, I can't wait to meet my first great grandchild."

Heaven smiled then looked at me. Those tears were beginning to develop again.

"We all are. What do you have on the menu for today?" I asked, changing the subject.

"I put on a roast and some baked chicken. Greens, mac and cheese, sweet potatoes, and cornbread."

"You went all out, didn't you?"

"You already know how I do," she laughed.

"Well, I definitely can't wait to eat," Heaven admitted.

"It's almost ready, we're just waiting on my cornbread. Y'all can go wash up."

I placed my hand on the small of Heaven's back and led her to the guest bathroom.

Before we ate, my grandmother made me say the prayer. She knew I was not into religion like that, but she always made me pray with her. I said a quick prayer and got it over with. Heaven was sitting there looking at me all surprised. We had not talked about religion to each other, so I guess it surprised her that I could pray. It wasn't something that I did on a regular basis, but I did know how.

"So Heaven," my mother started, "Saint tells us that you have other children."

"Yes two boys, Legend and King."

"How do they feel about Saint?"

"They love when Saint is around. They get to talk about sports and all that other stuff that I have no idea about."

"That's good," my grandmother added. "It's always a good sign when your kids like a man other than their father."

"I feel the same way."

"But how does their father feel about it. Saint told me that he has had some run-ins with him. My baby is on papers, and I don't need him going to jail behind no foolishness," my mother started.

I knew Sharon was going to come with the questions. She never tried to hold back from saying anything. I wish she had a filter like Instagram, but sometimes I was grateful for it. Like now, I was glad she made a point to tell Heaven I am still on papers. Heaven had no idea about how ignorant I could get. I wouldn't be that way toward her, but I would seriously hurt Flex. The only thing that kept me off of his ass was the fact that I was on papers, and the kids. I didn't want them seeing me be violent.

Like always, my grandmother swooped down and saved the day. She redirected the questions to Heaven and I. She was laying it on thick how much I loved her. It was all true, but I didn't want it to seem like I put her up to it. Heaven already knew how much I loved her; I made sure to tell and show her every day.

After we ate banana pudding for dessert, we retreated to the living room. My mother said she had something to do, so she left right after. I was happy she was finally leaving. That left all the people that actually had some sense there to talk, and have an educated conversation. All that shit she brought up about Flex was unnecessary. She was too nosey, and it was none of her business what was going on with Heaven and Flex. I was really sick of people bringing his name up around me.

It was getting late, and my grandmother began to yawn. She was usually in the bed by nine, so I know it was time for me to take Heaven home. I know she had to go get the boys, and I didn't want to keep her out late.

"Are you ready to go?" I asked Heaven.

"Whenever you are."

"It's getting late, and I know Maw Maw is getting sleepy."

"Okay."

"Thank you for dinner Maw Maw, it was tasty as usual."

"Anything for my Paw Paw."

"I know," I smiled, standing up from the sofa. "I'm going to run and take Heaven home."

"Alright. It was nice meeting you, Heaven. I look forward to meeting those boys."

"I will make sure to bring them next time."

"Okay, Paw you be careful out there on them dark streets."

"I will, see you in a little bit."

She walked us to the door as we turned to leave.

The ride to Heaven's house was fairly quiet. We talked, but I hadn't asked her the real questions. I wanted to know her honest opinion about my family. At the end of the day, we were stuck together for life. If she had any problems, I wanted to know now so that I could handle them. I didn't want three or four years to pass us by, then whatever became a big problem.

"What you think about my people, Heaven?"

"I love your Maw Maw, she is so sweet. And her food is to die for."

"So I'm taking it that you're not too fond of Sharon."

"She rubbed me the wrong way."

"Welcome to the club, she rubs everyone the wrong way. Don't worry about her though. She was never around for me, so I doubt she will be around for the baby. As long as you're cool with Maw, then that's fine with me. I consider her as my mother anyway."

"Yes, I love her."

"Me too," I smiled as I looked over at her. She reached over and interlocked her fingers in mine. I lifted her hand up to kiss it. For the remainder of the drive, I rode with her hand rested against my cheek. I so loved this woman, and I finally felt like we were headed in the right direction.

CHAPTER 9

Heaven

I bit my tongue with Saint's mother. I did not want to disrespect Saint or his grandmother's house, but Sharon was skating on thin ice. I knew that she was trying to get a rise out of me over dinner, but I was not going to stoop to her level. I had dealt with plenty of people like her in my lifetime, so I put on my sunglasses and handled her shade with class.

I spent the following day at work tying up loose ends before I started my extended maternity leave. I could have kept working because I was only about halfway through my pregnancy, but I wanted to enjoy the summer with my boys before they got a new brother or sister. I had plenty of money saved up and was earning money off of my investments, so it was not like I had to work at the moment. Plus, being around Saint's family made me miss my own. A trip back to South Carolina was a must. My parents owned a beach house in Myrtle Beach, so we all would be spending a month at the beach.

"Heaven, can you come to the teller stations please?" Lauren said through my intercom.

"I'll be right there," I responded. I had designated Lauren as my head teller; she would help my assistant manager with day to day tasks in my absence.

I finished up the email I was typing and locked my computer. The bank was fairly busy when I walked out onto the main floor. It was the lunch time rush and I could see the lines backing up. I hurried to the vacant teller window and opened it for the next customer. I did not see the next customer stepping to the window because I was logging into the computer, but when I looked up, I came face to face with the last person I wanted to see.

"Welcome to First National Bank. How may I help you?" I asked with a fake smile.

"Heaven, don't act like you don't know me," Kalina laughed. "How you been girl? I see you're getting big."

I rolled my eyes. I knew this bitch didn't come all the way here to make small talk. "Are you making a deposit or withdrawal today?"

"Damn, it's like that Heav?" Kalina asked, handing over a bank slip and some cash. "I'm making a deposit. My boyfriend gave me this so I can go shopping."

I bit down on my tongue. I could feel my temperature rising as I punched in Kalina's account information. I knew she was trying to bait me into asking who he was, but I already knew and it was taking all I had in me not to drag her over the counter and beat her ass. She just stood there with a stupid ass grin on her face. I did not know what it was with Flex and the bitches he chose, but these hoes were a few pancakes short of a stack. Damn, was I that stupid?

"Here you go, Miss Porter," I said with a tight smile as I handed her the receipt. "Is there anything else I can help you with?"

"No…we should go out to lunch girl," she smiled at me.

"I'm good," I said flatly. "You have a good day. Next please."

I shut her down quick and sent her packing. Kalina was so desperate to floss in front of me and make me jealous. I guess she did not realize that all of the banks were linked and I could see that she pulled the exact amount from one branch only to come deposit it here. That bitch tried it. I finished helping thin out the line and took my lunch break. My feet were hurting and I was tempted to take the rest of the day off, but since my doctor's appointment was the next day I decided to stick it out.

I grabbed my purse and keys from my office before I headed out to find me something to eat, and to clear my head. I do not know why Kalina and Flex being together bothered me so much. I knew what type of man Flex was, and that he was not a prize. Kalina could have that stress if she wanted it. I needed to put things in perspective and realize what I had in Saint. He was working on a job in DeSoto, so I decided to swing by and bring him lunch too. Knowing him, he probably did not plan on taking a lunch break. Plus, I missed him even though I had just seen him the night before.

"What are you doing here?" Saint smiled when I pulled up to his job site.

"I brought you lunch," I said, holding up the bag from the sandwich shop I had stopped at on the way. I tried to put on a smile, but my mind was still on Kalina.

"What's wrong with you?" Saint asked me with a raised eyebrow as he took the bag from me. I do not know how he did it, but he was pretty good at seeing right through me.

"I saw Kalina today."

"Okay and?"

"She came in the bank fronting like her 'boyfriend' had given her money to shop with," I said, using air quotes.

"I don't see why that has you upset."

"She tried to fucking play me."

"Do you still have feelings for Flex?"

"No…I just…when you have someone you trusted go behind your back and do some shady shit like that…it just irks my soul, okay?"

"You got plenty of other things to worry about."

Saint was right. We were about to be bringing a baby into the world in a few short months. I needed to focus my attention on that, and stop worrying about what Kalina had going on with Flex. I could not help but to wonder if he really was giving her money though. If he was, that money could have been going to his kids and not some thot who fucked everybody's man. The wheels in my head started to turn and I came up with the only possible solution I could think of to make sure that my kids were taken care of.

"I think I'm going to put Flex up for child support," I said, looking up at Saint. The look on his face told me that I had chosen the wrong words to say.

"You just sound like a bitter baby mama now."

"I'm not," I said, crossing my arms.

"What is it about this nigga that keep you in your feelings like this?"

"I'm just hurt."

"Exactly the reason why that's the wrong move. You hurt. That pregnancy must really be fucking with your brain because I thought you were smarter than this."

"If he givin' out money...his kids deserve it too," I said, crossing my arms.

"I'm not saying they don't, but Heav you aren't exactly hurting for money and neither am I. If those two want to be together, let them be together and we will worry about us."

I saw where Saint was coming from. I just could not get over it. I was like a toddler with my toys. If I played with it before, it was mine. I also knew that if I wanted to keep my relationship with Saint on track, I was gonna have to let this shit go. Saint was right. Neither one of us was hurting for money. I was just wanting to do some bitter baby mama shit.

"Are you still coming to my appointment in the morning?" I asked, hoping to change the subject.

"Of course. I would not miss it."

"I just wanted to drop lunch off for you," I smiled. "I missed you."

Saint kissed me deeply through the window, making me wish that we could spend the rest of the day in bed making another baby. It made me forget about the fucked up morning I had experienced. We said our goodbyes and I headed back to work with a huge smile on my face. The rest of the day went by smoothly. It was like Saint's kisses had worked magic. Hell, I think his kisses cleared five o'clock traffic for me. I was able to pick up the kids and get home in a decent amount of time.

I should have known that my good time would be short lived because when I pulled at my house, Flex was in my driveway waiting on me. It's like he and Kalina had both decided to fuck up my day. I did not know why he was at my house, because I had made it clear that he was no longer welcomed the last time he caused issues between Saint and I. I watched him as he stepped out of the car and approached my window.

"Daddy!" the boys yelled from the back seat. I rolled my eyes because no matter how much this nigga neglected his kids, they still loved him.

I opened my car door, causing Flex to step back. I wish I could have hit him with my car, but hitting him with the door would have to do. I grabbed my purse from the passenger seat and got out.

"Come on boys," I said, opening the door for King.

"You not gonna speak?" Flex asked as I walked to my front door.

"Why? What do you want?"

"I came to see my kids."

"Well, that does not require me speaking to you," I snorted. "You can stand outside and talk to them. Boys, bring your book bags in the house and get your ball so you can play with your daddy."

The boys shot past me as I opened my front door and ran up the stairs. They had to change out of their school uniforms before they could go out to play, so that left Flex and I alone at the front door. I did not want him in my house, so I held the door partially closed.

"We need to talk, Heaven."

"I don't have anything to say to you."

"You been keeping my boys from me."

"You keep too much drama going on, and don't start acting like you care now. You don't even take care of *your* boys."

"You sound so bitter. That nigga left you stuck with another baby and you taking it out on me."

"*My man* did not leave me stuck with anything. You tried to break us up and failed. I'm moving the fuck on and building a family with a man who loves me," I said, rubbing my belly to add emphasis.

"You ain't gonna keeps my kids away from me, Heaven," Flex said, taking a step toward me. I backed into the house.

"You need to stay outside, Flex," I warned.

"Fuck that. What are you going to do?"

"Don't worry about what I'm going to do. I would worry about what Saint will do if he catches you up in here again. You should be tired of getting your ass beat by him."

Flex chuckled and took a step back. I knew that his ass was scared. I do not know how he survived in the streets if he could get his ass beat so easily.

"That's another thing…you keep having that violent ass nigga around my kids, I'm gonna file for custody."

My heart dropped. Even though I knew that Flex did not have a case or the means to support the kids, the thought of having my boys taken from me scared me. I wanted to fight his ass right there on my front porch, but I had to remember I was pregnant and he was stronger than me.

"Boys, stay in the house," I said without taking my eyes off of Flex. I could hear the boys voice their disappointment. "You can think you can take my kids all you want to, but I will be dead and it will be a cold day in Hell before you do that."

"All that can be arranged, Heav. I think that nigga done gave you a false sense of security and you done forgot who you dealing with. If you continue to keep my kids away from me…I will get custody."

I smiled because Flex really had me fucked up, and he forgot who my daddy was. He forgot who my man was. Most importantly, he did not know what he was getting into fucking with a real mother. I would protect my kids by any means necessary, and he could try to drag me into a custody battle but he would surely come out on the wrong end. I had completely forgotten about him and Kalina by then. He had crossed a whole 'nother line that had me on fire.

"I'd like to see you try. Goodbye Flex," I smiled as I closed the door.

CHAPTER 10

Saint

When Heaven called me crying about Flex, my patience was beginning to run thin—not just with Flex, but with Heaven also. She was always so strong when it came to me, but weak as a wet paper bag when it came to him. He only did and said shit that pissed her off, I know that much. I didn't like that fact that he still had that kind effect or control over her. After all of the years she had dealt with him, she should have learned to ignore his threats by now. He didn't want them damn kids, he wanted Heaven's ass. From what she has told me, he had never been a great father. What the fuck would make her think that he wanted them full time?

Since Heaven was so upset, I left work heading straight to her house. She was upset and I didn't want her to be. Above anything else, I still wanted to make sure she was alright. She was carrying my baby, and I didn't want her stressed out. If something happened to my baby I swear, Heaven and Flex would be in trouble. I pulled into the driveway behind Heaven's ride, and quickly jumped out. I could hear the boys playing basketball in the backyard, so I entered the yard through the

71

back gate.

I stood there watching as Legend and King played a game of one on one. Even though King was smaller than Legend, he still had skills. That's what playing with an older brother would get you. It made you have to play harder in order to attempt to win. Legend spotted me standing there and started in my direction.

"What's up, Saint," he spoke.

"What's going on, big man. Hey lil' man," I said, speaking to King as he approached us.

"Hey Saint," King spoke, giving me a hug.

"Y'all alright?"

"Yes," they both said in unison.

"But my mama is sad," King revealed to me. "My daddy made her cry."

Legend looked at me, "He said he is going to take us away."

That pissed me off even more. The fact that all of this bullshit was happening in front of the boys was even worse. I don't know why she didn't just leave when she saw him, or slam the door when he began to talk nonsense.

"Don't worry about it," I assured them. "Everything will be alright."

"Can you make Mama happy again, Saint?" Legend asked.

"I will. Finish playing while I go talk to mama."

They both ran off, and I started toward the back door.

The house was still and quiet when I entered. I grabbed a bottle of water out the fridge, then began to look for Heaven. She wasn't downstairs, so she had to be in the bedroom. I chugged my water as I climbed the stairs. The vomiting made me dehydrated, so I drank water all day. When we went to the doctor, I would make sure to ask if there was something I could do about it.

Heaven was lying on her back in the bed when I walked inside the room. Her eyes were closed, so I assumed she was sleep. I walked over to her side quietly, and sat down next to her. She opened her eyes just as I was placing my hand on her belly.

"Hey baby, are you alright?"

"Yes, I'm alright. Flex just had my blood boiling for a minute."

"Stop letting him do that to you. He is only doing shit that he knows will piss you off. You're just falling right into his little traps. Do you really think he will file for full custody of the boys?"

"I don't know. Flex is silly like that, so I wouldn't put it past him."

"But you know damn well no judge in Texas will give him full custody. For what? He would have to prove that you are an unfit mother before the state of Texas will do that."

"He brought you up, and the fact that you are violent toward him. He said if you're around his boys, he will file."

"Heaven listen, I know my background will stop be from doing a lot of things, but it won't get the boys taken away from you. Yes, I have a record, but I haven't been in any trouble in years. I am what the state would call rehabilitated. I got out and made something of myself. Plus, you're having my child, so he can't stop me from being around."

"I understand that much, but he doesn't seem to."

"That's alright, he will sooner or later."

She laid there looking at the ceiling as if she was thinking. Hopefully, she would take my advice and stop letting Flex upset her. I'd broken the law enough times to know the laws. No judge that's even out of their mind would give Flex full custody. Heaven was a great mother and there was nothing for her to worry about.

Since Heaven was in a mood, I went downstairs to figure out what we would eat for dinner. She hadn't taken anything out, so I guess I would go pick something up. I had a taste for crab legs and hot wings. If I didn't know any better, I would think I was carrying the baby. I had morning sickness, I slept anytime I was still for more than 10 minutes, not to mention out of this world cravings.

I called the Shell Shack and placed an order for pick up. It wasn't going to take long for to the order to get ready, so I called the boys inside. They were all sweaty from playing ball, and I sent then to get cleaned up. I was going to take them with me to pick up the food while Heaven rested. She needed a little alone time, and it gave me time to talk to the boys. They had seen and heard a lot, so I wanted to know how they felt about everything.

Ж

After checking the messages at the office, I got my things together and left. Today, we were going to find out the sex of the baby. I was overly excited to find out what had been baking these past few months. I didn't have a preference on what it would be. A healthy baby was just fine with me. My grandmother seemed to believe that it was a girl. She said that was the reason why I had all of the pregnancy symptoms. I was fine with a girl since Heaven had two boys already.

Heaven and I both had to go back to work afterward, so I was meeting her at the doctor's office. When I pulled into the parking lot, I saw Heaven's car was already there. There was an empty spot next to her that I pulled into. She was still seated inside looking in the mirror. I tapped the horn to get her attention. She looked at me and smiled as I stepped out of the truck. I hit the lock button, then walked over to open her door.

"Good morning, baby," I spoke.

"Morning Saint."

"Are you excited?"

"Of course I am. I've been waiting on this day for a month."

"Me too. I know we haven't really discussed it, but what do you want it to be?"

"A girl, I already have two rough boys. I want a mini-me to dress up, and to go shop with. The boys don't like doing either of those things, and I'm tired of hearing about sports all the time."

I laughed, "I know you are, but I hope it's another boy," I joked.

"Please Lord, let it be a girl," she begged.

"Well let's go see."

I took her by the hand, and we strolled toward the office.

While Heaven went to sign in, I found us some seats. I looked around at all of the big belly women sitting in the waiting area. Most of them were there without a man on their side. I didn't know their situation, but I felt sorry for them being there alone. No woman should have to go through this process alone. It takes two to make a baby, and two people should step up and take responsibility.

It took about thirty minutes for them to call Heaven's name. I didn't understand the point of an appointment if they weren't going to stick to that time. With each minute that went past our scheduled time, I grew more anxious. Once we got to the back, we were still waiting on the sonographer. The room door finally swung open, and my heart began to beat triple time. This was going to be the first time that I was going to get a glimpse of my seed.

I held Heaven's hand while the sonographer prepared the tray and machine. We both had smiles on our faces as we waited in anticipation. I swear, it seemed like the sonographer was moving in slow motion. I wasn't aware of the procedure, so I wasn't really sure. Patience and I weren't best friends, and it could all just be in my head. Through it all, I held my composure and maintained calm.

Heaven's eyes as well as my own were glued to the monitor. The sonographer pointed out each limb of the baby to us. I'm glad she did, because the only thing I recognized is the head.

"What do you guys want the sex to be?" the sonographer asked.

"I want it to be a girl because I have boys already," Heaven answered. "But of course he wants a boy."

"No, I just want a healthy baby."

"So far so good heath wise. The baby seems to be growing at the appropriate rate according to due date."

"What's the sex?" I impatiently asked.

She laughed, "Okay, I know that's what you really want to know. You guys will be welcoming a baby girl into the world."

Heaven and I looked at each other at the same time. We both had smiles on our faces, her even more than me. I leaned over and gave her a kiss. Tears of joy were streaming down her face toward her ears. I grabbed a napkin to dab them off.

"Are you happy Saint?"

"Of course I am, baby. I can't wait to spoil our princess."

"Me too, and I can't wait to tell the boys. They both want a little sister."

"Well, looks like everyone has gotten what they wanted."

"Here you go," the sonographer said, laying some napkins on Heaven's belly. "You can use these to wipe away the gel."

I placed my hand on the napkins, and proceeded to wipe her belly off. Once I removed all of the gel, I leaned over and kissed her belly. Knowing that I had a daughter on the way did something to me. I had to be there for my daughter one hundred percent of the time. There were no if's, and's, or but's about that. Now it was time for us to talk about what we are going to do.

CHAPTER 11

Heaven

Saint was right, I needed to stop letting Flex upset me. He just had a gift for getting under my skin. I had to start taking the things he did with a grain of salt for the sake of my baby girl. Saint also put me on game letting me know that the boys had heard Flex say that he would take them from me. That shit really pissed me off. One thing I did not play about was my kids.

I needed a break from the drama that was going on in my life, and school ending could not have come at a better time. I was ready to go home to South Carolina and let my mommy dote on me. I had not been home since King was about three, so this trip was long overdue. We were flying directly into Myrtle Beach, and my father would be picking the boys and I up from the airport. Saint was not happy about me leaving so soon after us getting back together, but I had already planned the trip and I missed my parents. I did invite him to come spend a couple of weeks with us. Our beach house was six bedrooms, so there was plenty of space.

"I still don't see why you gotta go for a month," Saint said, watching me pack.

"I miss my parents, and I haven't been home in four years. Plus, it's just so relaxing at the beach. You can come down as soon as you figure out who can take over for you. I want you to meet my parents, and it can be a vacation before the baby comes. It will be like a babymoon."

"Babymoon? Who came up with that bullshit?"

"Don't be like that," I laughed. "All it means is it is a vacation before the baby arrives. It's a time to unwind and relax. This may be your first, but I've been to this rodeo and it's a lot of sleepless nights and diapers."

The thought alone made me shudder. I could not believe that I was starting over all over again. Potty training King had been a task. He was not fully trained until he was almost three. I heard girls were easier, so I prayed it was true.

"How many dresses are you going to take?" Saint asked, going through my suitcase. He had already thrown my two-piece out saying I did not need to wear a bikini. He was starting to get on my nerves.

"I'm comfortable in sundresses. They're not tight around my stomach and they are easy to put on and match with flip flops. I'm starting to lose sight of my feet," I said, easing down on the bed. I had gained more weight at this stage in my pregnancy than I did with my two previous pregnancies. In fact, I did not start showing with my previous ones until the last couple of months.

"Let me find out you at the beach getting niggas to look at your ass."

"Don't nobody want my pregnant ass, but you."

"I wish you weren't going, but I understand," Saint said, kissing me on my forehead.

"You'll be down to visit in a couple of weeks. It won't be long and we can video chat," I said. I was seriously having second thoughts about going because I knew that I would be missing Saint something serious.

"What time does your flight leave again?"

"7:15 in the morning. We need to be at the airport by six. I'm gonna pre-check our bags since it's just clothes. We'll get toiletries once when we get there," I said, checking my bag to make sure that I had packed everything. I also made mental note to buy a new swimsuit once I landed as well.

"Well, I'm just going to stay here with you tonight," Saint said, grabbing his meat. I instantly knew exactly what he had planned for our last night together. I was game for it.

Ж

Stepping off the plane was a bittersweet moment for me. I was happy to be back in South Carolina, but I missed Saint already. I had to keep reminding myself that he would be here as soon as he tied up loose ends back home. My parents were excited to meet him. Even though we had the hiccup in our relationship, I never spoke bad about Saint and I let them know that our break up was because of Flex's refusal to let go. I held King by the hand as Legend and I pulled our luggage from the carousel.

"Let me get that for you, baby girl," my heart melted at the sound of my father's voice in my ear. I had to fight the tears because I was a true daddy's girl.

My father, David Santana, was of Dominican descent. He met my mother, Jubilee, while he was studying for his law degree at the University of South Carolina. She was an undergrad student studying education. My mother was a preacher's kid, which is how she got the name Jubilee, and how I ended up being named Heaven. The story went that my grandmother looked me right in the face and said that I looked like a little piece of Heaven. The name stuck, needless to say.

"Hey Daddy," I said, hugging him tight. My father was tall so my head still rested easily on his chest.

He stood at about six feet four inches tall with a salt and pepper goatee. My father always looked like he had been kissed by the sun with his bronze skin. To be in his fifties, he was still in shape. My father looked more like my older brother than my parent.

"Papa!" the boys yelled as they jumped into his arms.

"My boys," he laughed as he hugged them tightly. He looked at me as the smile radiated in his eyes.

"I hear I have a granddaughter coming soon," he smiled.

"Yep. This will be the last one too," I laughed.

"Nonsense, you should have a large family. I always regretted only having one child."

"I didn't," I smiled. I loved being the only child.

"Well let's get going," he said, taking my suitcase from me. We walked the short distance to the loading area where his Mercedes was parked.

We rode through the city toward North Myrtle Beach. I made a mental note of the restaurants I wanted to eat at. My mother was also an excellent cook, so I definitely would be at her dinner table. The ride to the beach house was filled with laughter and the kids updating papa on everything that was going on back in Dallas. My parents hated that I lived so far away. I had even contemplated moving back home, but I had made a life for myself in Dallas and it was out of the question. When we pulled up to the house, my mother was standing on her expansive front porch waiting for me.

I looked like a spitting image of her mother. My mother was a petite woman with caramel skin and shoulder length hair that had been dyed honey blonde and cut into a stylish bob. I had my father's hair texture and eye color, but everything else came courtesy of Jubilee Santana. My mother was a true beauty, and the definition of black not cracking. She was dressed in a chiffon sundress and large straw sunhat, looking like she had just stepped off of a vacation advertisement.

"My baby!" Jubilee smiled, coming off of the porch to greet me.

"Hey Mama," I said, hugging her back.

"Consuela is going to take the boys to the beach because we need to talk," my mother whispered in my ear. Consuela was my father's sister. She came up from the Dominican Republic to visit.

"Boys, come on and let's get your swim trunks. Titi Consuela is going to take you to the beach," I called. The boys did not need to be told twice. They were dressed and out the door in record time.

My parent's beach house had three floors with elevator access. They occupied the top floor bedrooms with Consuela while the boys and I would stay on the second floor. My mother had recently had the entire house renovated and it looked like a five-star resort. The home had been in our family since my father made partner at his law firm over twenty years ago. He was a high-profile defense attorney.

"Let's talk," my mother said, watching Consuela lead the boys down the path that lead to our private portion of beach. We sat out on the porch to enjoy the air.

"Can't we do this another time?" I asked yawning.

"No time is better than the present. So, this fool really thinks I would allow him to get custody of my grandbabies?"

"That's what his mind is set on."

"And you're letting it stress you out while you're pregnant with my granddaughter?"

I nodded my head slightly. "Saint assured me that he would not get custody."

"Saint is right. I like him. The only way any judge would grant that lowlife custody is if you were an unfit mother. I raised you, and I know you are anything but one. Don't let that dumb ass get under your skin because he sees you're happy and wants to ruin it. I can tell that Saint makes you happy because you're glowing now, and by how heartbroken you were over your fight."

I smiled because my mother was right. Saint made me happy and it made everyone around us jealous. I was my own worst enemy when it came to believing the mind games that Flex was playing with me. It was time that I fought fire with fire, and I was with the right man to help me do it…my father.

CHAPTER 12

Saint

After I dropped Heaven and the boys off at the airport, I headed over to the bank. Michelle told me that I won the bid and was approved for the house. I had to go get a cashier's check for the down payment. I hadn't mentioned the new house to Heaven, but since it would be mine I needed to tell her about it. We were supposed to get a place together before everything went sour. I wanted for her and the boys to move in the new house to avoid Flex being able to pop up. That was a conversation that we needed to have very soon.

When I walked into the bank, I felt like royalty. Everyone made it a point to speak to me, and I didn't have to wait in line. The lead teller opened her line just to assist me. I was grateful for that because I had a yard consultation in two hours. That would cut at least 10 minutes that I would have wasted in line. While the teller printed out my check, I turned back to look at Heaven's office. I know she isn't there, but I did it out of habit.

I pulled away from the bank with the truck on two wheels. I wanted to reach Michelle as soon as possible so that I would have time to pick up some breakfast before the consultation. This was the first day in week that I hadn't regurgitated when I woke up. Heaven's doctor prescribed me a pill for nausea, and it finally started to work. It didn't do anything about the cravings, but that I could deal with. Eating was something that I enjoyed, so I didn't want to fuck with that anyway.

Michelle was standing outside of the house when I pulled up. Last time I parked on the street, but today I pulled into the driveway. Officially it was mine, even though I hadn't signed on the dotted line yet. I couldn't wait to sign the papers. I killed the engine and jumped out.

"Good morning, Saint."

"Great morning, Michelle," I smiled.

"Well yes" she laughed. "It is a great morning for you."

"For you too."

She gave me a bashful smile, then waved for me to follow her. I walked behind Michelle all the way into the kitchen. She had all of the documents already laid out with a pen to sign laying on top. I was sure that I would sign the contract, but I was also going to take my time and read through the paperwork. I was no fool, and I read everything that I signed my name on. I almost got caught up in signing one of those bullshit mortgage loans with my last home. I was no fool then, and I was even wiser now.

It took me a while, but I read every word on every page. My credit was where it needed to be, so my interest rate was lower than I thought it would be. Today was definitely turning out better than it started. I didn't want Heaven and the boys to leave without me. She was persistent about going now, so I had to let her leave. A month was a long time to be gone, and I planned to go visit for a week or two. Once I got everything situated in Dallas, I would join them.

"Does everything look fine?" Michelle asked, interrupting my thoughts.

"Yes it does." I reached in my back pocket and pulled out the envelope containing the check. "Here you go."

She took it from me, then I began to sign each document. Once I laid the pen down, Michelle handed over the keys to me.

"Here you go, Saint. You are now a homeowner, again."

I smiled. "Thanks Michelle."

"You're welcome. And if you know anyone else in need of a home, give them my card."

"I sure will."

"Alright, let me get out of here and get this paperwork to the bank."

I didn't have a reason to stay, so I walked out behind her. It was thirty minutes until the consultation, and it looked like I would have to wait until afterward to grab a bite to eat.

The consultation didn't take long at all. Everything that the owner wanted was pretty basic. I could get a few of the new guys to start on it tomorrow. The work wouldn't take more than two days, so I would come out to assist them with it. Now that the consultation was done, it was time to fill my belly. With Heaven and the boys gone, I was feeling alone. I send Jug a text message to see if he wanted to eat with me. He was down, so I told him to meet me at Johnathan's in Oak Cliff.

Johnathan's was a house on Beckley that had been turned into a restaurant. The food they served was awesome. You could tell that everything was home cooked, and they stayed packed. Anytime they were open, you could pass by and see a line of people waiting to get seated. It was now lunch time, so I knew the line would probably be long. It didn't matter because neither one of us were on a schedule.

As I jumped out of my truck, I saw Jug's car pull into the lot. I stood next to my truck to wait on him. Jug swung his car into the spot and stepped out.

"What's up nigga?" Jug spoke.

"Ain't shit bro," I dapped him up. "Trying to fill my belly."

"It looks like you've done that enough."

"What you mean?"

"You gaining weight."

"For real?" I asked, looking down at myself.

"Yup," he laughed and patted my stomach. "I thought Heaven was having the baby, my nigga."

"Fuck you lil' bastard. Nah but for real, am I gaining weight?"

"Muthafucka I done said yeah," he laughed. "Come on, let's go eat."

I walked next to him, but still thinking about me gaining weight. If I had, it had to be noticeable for him to say something. I'd always worn my clothes big, so I couldn't tell by the fit.

The wait wasn't as long as I expected. We were seated five minutes after we signed in. Since I still had the weight gain on my mind, I ordered an omelet. I had my mouth set on chicken and waffles, but I passed on it. Starting tomorrow, I would be back in the gym.

"So are you excited about the lil' one?" Jug asked.

"Hell yeah, but I'm nervous. I don't know how to do shit with no baby."

"All you gotta do it keep they ass fed."

"How would you know, you don't even have kids."

"But all the bitches I fuck with do. Feed and change their ass, and you'll be good."

"I don't even know how to change a diaper."

"You'll figure it out nigga. I have faith in you," he smirked.

"What the fuck ever," I laughed.

The waitress walked up with our food, and cut that conversation short. I was ready to end it anyway. One thing that I did realize was that I had a lot to learn before baby girl got here. Heaven had a lot to teach me because I wanted to be hands on. She had practically raised the boys alone, and I wanted to take the weight off of her with mine.

After having lunch with Jug, I headed over to Heaven's condo. Since she was going to be gone for an extended period, I told her I would stay over. She stayed in a nice neighborhood, but that's exactly where thieves went to steal. I knew because I used to be one of them. Not only that, I would have peace and quiet at Heaven's place. I loved my grandmother, but she didn't let me rest how I wanted to. She wanted me to wake up early even on my days off.

Walking into Heaven's quiet house alone made me feel different. I had never been in there alone besides a few hours here and there. It was a little warm, so I pushed the air down. After eating that meal, I was in need of a quick nap. I wouldn't be able to sleep well if it was too warm. I climbed the stairs and kicked my shoes off at the bedroom door. The bed was made up, so I laid on top on the comforter.

The chiming of the doorbell woke me from my nap. I looked at the time and it was almost two. I stretched, then drug myself out of the bed. Before opening the door, I took a look out of the window. I saw that Flex's car was sitting out front, so I hurried to open the door.

"What?" I asked, swinging the door open.

"Where the fuck is Heaven?"

"She's not here."

"Why you here if she's not here? You stay here now?"

"Yeah, you got a problem with that? I heard you've been doing a lot of talkin' about me, but you ain't said shit to me. My nigga if you got some shit to get off yo' chest, I suggest you do it now 'cause I ain't going nowhere."

"We gon' see about that."

"No we not. I'm tellin' yo' ass now that I am here to stay, so state yo' business for being here."

"I'm trying to see my boys, but Heaven won't answer her damn phone."

"Well they're on vacation right now. They won't be back for another month or so."

"You tell that bitch…"

Pow. I stole him right in his mouth midsentence.

"When you speak about the mother of my child, you better refrain from calling her a bitch, my nigga. That disrespectful shit stops now." He looked up at me, then swung at me off balance. I weaved to the side and cocked my right fist all the way back. He thought he was gon' weave my punch, but I swung with the left. He leaned right into it, and went flying down the stairs on the porch. "Fuck nigga, if you come back around here with that bullshit, I'm gon' put a bullet in yo' ass! You feel me?"

"That's exactly why I don't want my fuckin' kids around yo' ass."

"I don't give a fuck what you want. You not even around yo' kids, how the fuck you gon' tell me not to be around them? At the end of the day, Heaven is my baby mama too, so I'm here to stay. If you can take an ass whoopin' every time you come over with that silly shit, I have no problem with delivering it. What the fuck you wanna do, bitch ass nigga?"

He stood up from the ground and mugged me. "This shit ain't over."

"You damn right it ain't 'cause Heaven knows that you're fuckin' Kalina." He looked at me like how you know. "Yeah she knows, and I've kept her off y'all ass about it. You'll be better off being on your best behavior right now."

"Well you tell Heaven that she better call me back ASAP."

"I'm not tellin' her to call you. I'm sure she sees that you've called already."

He looked for a second, then turned to walk to his car. I stood there watching his every move. He jumped into his car and sped off. I grabbed my phone from my pocket to call Heaven. I had to let her know what just happened in case she decided to answer Flex's calls. I'm sure that little scuffle would have him in his feelings, and he was going to act like a bitch even more.

CHAPTER 13

Heaven

$\mathcal{I}$f it was not one thing, it was another. Saint called me to fill me in on Flex coming to the house. Of course, he got his ass beat. I knew that he had been calling me, but I was on vacation and did not have time for his bullshit. Saint also told me that he spilled the beans about me knowing about him being with Kalina. Flex getting his ass beat again was sure to cause problems, so I definitely had to move faster with my plan.

My father was out golfing with some friends, so I would have to wait until he returned to talk to him. Even though I had full physical custody of my boys, I wanted to have it legally put on paper because Flex was being real reckless. I sat holding my phone in my hand contemplating my next move when it chimed, letting me know that I got a text.

KALINA: You need to stop tripping and let me see my step kids.

I read over the text two more times. *This bitch has hit her head, I* thought to myself. I did not bother to respond. She did not deserve an answer, but I knew that Flex told her that I had found out about them.

She was trying to rub that shit in my face but if she knew like I knew, Flex was not a catch.

I guess when I did not respond to her text, Kalina decided to up the ante by taking her beef to Facebook. My phone started to go crazy with notifications. I opened the app and looked through my notifications. Kalina had tagged me in a post. It had already gotten a few comments.

Kalina Marie 8 mins ago- If somebody see *Heaven Santana* around Dallas tell her to stop tripping and let my bae see his kids.

I read a lot of "she wrong" and "I hate females like that" comments before I decided to comment. It was completely out of my character to do something like that, but I had enough of Kalina.

Heaven Santana Any bitch that lay up with a nigga that got kids & watch him be an ain't shit dad is an ain't shit bitch. Ya'll make a perfect couple.

After I commented, I unfollowed the post so I would not get any more notifications. I posted a few pictures of my sonogram and pictures of Saint and I. If she wanted to be stupid, I was going to show her how happy I was. You block haters with happiness. I did not stay logged on for long because I did not want to get too involved with Kalina or her drama. I was also happy that Saint did not do Facebook so that he would not try and check me on what I had done.

"Heaven, you have a delivery baby," my mother called from the front door. I got up to see what it was.

I was smiling from ear to ear; my daddy had bought home steamed blue crabs from Mr. Fish. He knew I loved that place. I could eat half a dozen by myself. My mother thought it would be a good idea for us to eat outside so the smell would not stick around in the house. We had a picnic table on our elevated backyard with a clear view of the ocean. It was the perfect backdrop to enjoy the crabs.

"So when are we going to meet this Saint, hija?" my father asked.

"He's going to get things situated with his landscaping business and make sure his employees are situated, and then he will be here."

"How does he feel about you having kids already?" I knew that my father would come with the third degree. I was glad he was doing it with me instead of with Saint.

"He loves the boys. They get along well."

My dad nodded approvingly. He asked me if I saw myself marrying Saint. I told him that I did not know. I knew that my parents did not agree with me having kids out of wedlock, but marriage was never something I really thought of. If Saint asked, I might accept, but I was happy with how our relationship was going at the present. There were plenty of couples who had been together for years and never married, so I did not see why we could not be like those couples.

Ж

When Saint had finally called me to tell me that he was flying into Myrtle Beach, I was like a kid waiting on Christmas. The day had finally arrived and I was super excited. I missed Saint something terrible. His flight was due to land around ten in the morning, so I got up around eight to get dressed and head to the airport. Traffic was kind of heavy with locals on their way to work, which caused me to make it just in time. I stood outside of my daddy's Mercedes and waited for Saint to come out of the sliding doors.

I could not contain my smile when I saw him come through those doors. Saint had put on some weight during my pregnancy, but it looked like he had been working out to get rid of it. I figured one of his workers or Jug had pointed it out to him. I was not going to because I was happy someone besides myself was gaining weight.

"Hey baby," I said, greeting him with a deep kiss. I felt his strong arms wrap around my body and hug me tight.

"I missed you."

"I missed you too, baby. I'm so glad you came out."

"I hope you didn't think I was gonna be away from my woman and baby for a whole month," he smirked. I giggled and grabbed him by the hand, leading him to the car. "Damn Heav, your parents doing it big."

"Nigga we on the same level," I punched him in the shoulder.

"We don't own vacation homes," Saint said as we got in the car. I pulled away from the curb.

"Actually…I own a condo in the Dominican Republic where my family is from."

"Damn Heav, you keeping secrets?"

"No, it's nothing like that. I just never got around to it. I mean, I don't know your whole financial situation. The condo was a college graduation gift from my father. He sent me to the DR when I graduated high school, and I loved it down there so much he bought it for me when I graduated college."

"Oh, so you're spoiled."

"You already knew that," I laughed, "but you also know I work for mine. Daddy taught me how to invest, and my money makes money."

"That's what's up. I got to meet the man who raised such a smart and beautiful daughter."

I blushed hard. Even though he complimented me all the time, Saint still made me feel special. We drove through the city and I showed him all of my favorite places. He was blown away when we pulled up to my parents' home. He said it looked like it belonged on a magazine cover. I told him that it had been on the cover of one of the local magazines.

"Come on so you can meet my parents," I said, grabbing him by the hand.

My parents and the boys were all seated at the kitchen table eating the brunch that my Titi Consuela had prepared. Looking at the table, I could see that she had made all of my father's favorite dishes from the Dominican Republic, as well as some American favorites. Brunch with my family was a lot less stressful than it had been when we had dinner with Saint's family. We laughed and ate like one big happy family. My mother was smitten with Saint. He turned on his charm and he had her eating out of the palm of his hand. My father was impressed with Saint's business sense and how attentive he was to me.

"Saint, we must get out and talk man to man about my daughter," my father said after brunch. "Take a walk with me, son."

"Daddy…don't go running him off," I warned.

"Nonsense, hija. I just want to pick his brain. You're my only child, so I have to make sure you're in good hands."

"It's cool Heav," Saint gave me a smile.

"Daddy, don't go telling him embarrassing stories…I know how you can get."

"Relax," my mother said, laying a hand on her arm. "It will be fine."

Saint and my father were gone for an hour. They came back laughing and joking. I wanted to know what they had talked about and Saint would not tell me. I pouted for the rest of the day. My mother laughed at how much of a brat I was being, but she understood.

"Your family is cool, Heav," Saint said, holding me in bed later that night.

"I'm glad you like them," I said, turning my back to him so he could wrap his arms around my stomach.

"I like you too," he said, kissing the back of my neck.

"I love you," I said, pressing my ass into his hardening manhood.

No more words were spoken as Saint lifted my nightgown and exposed my bare ass. I felt his hand rub over it before he slid inside of me. I tried to be quiet. Even though my parents were on another floor, the kids were right next door and I did not want to wake them. Saint delivered strong, slow, and sensual thrusts, making me leak all over him and the bed. I moaned softly as he brought me to my peak. My g-spot was extra sensitive due to my pregnancy, so I could cum back to back with no issue.

"Fuck," I heard Saint gasp as he sped his strokes up. I bit down into the pillow to keep from crying out. Saint spilled his seed inside of me. If I had not been pregnant, we would have definitely made a baby that night. Saint kissed the back of my neck again and within seconds, he was asleep. I drifted off to sleep listening to Saint's light snores, completely satisfied with my man.

CHAPTER 14

Saint

When I opened my eyes, the sun was starting to rise. Heaven was sleeping peacefully with her head on my chest. Since we were in her parent's home, I eased out the bed to get myself together. Even though it was obvious that we are sexually active, I didn't want to be disrespectful. Mrs. Santana was very Christian-like, and I didn't want to be seen laid up in their home with Heaven. Not only that, the boys had never seen Heaven in me in the bed under the covers together. When I saw my mother in the bed with a man for the first time, it did something to me as a boy. I didn't want to give them that same feeling I had back then.

As I emerged from the bathroom, I could smell breakfast being made. My stomach instantly began to growl. I'm not sure what was being cooked, but it smelled good as hell. I threw my night clothes in my suitcase and zipped it up. When I looked up, Heaven was sitting up in the bed looking at me.

"Morning, sleepy head," I spoke.

"Hey. What are you doing up so early?"

"Don't you smell food cooking?" I asked.

"You're sounding real greedy right now," she laughed.

"I know, but your father is taking the boys and I to fish after breakfast."

"Oh okay. I guess I'll go ahead and get up too. My mother has an entire day planned for us also."

I walked over towards the bed and sat down next to her. "You mean to tell me we are going to go another day without being around each other? Seems like we are seeing less of each other here."

"My father just wants to get to know you better. And my mother, well she misses me."

"I understand that, but I want you by my side. I didn't come all the way here to kick it with your dad. I mean he's cool and all, but I don't want to rub and kiss up on him."

She laughed. "It's just a few hours, Saint. Tomorrow we can go do something with the boys."

"That sounds more like it."

Heaven looked at me, then down at my shoes. "You're going to fish in your Gucci sneaks?"

"Well I didn't bring anything to get dirty in. It'll be alright; if not, I'll get another pair." I leaned over and kissed her. "Get up and get dressed. I'll go get the boys up."

"Alright, and make sure King takes a shower. He will try to skip out on it like he did last night."

"We're going fishing. He can take one afterward."

"Saint."

"What? He's a boy, he will be alright for a few hours. You know he is going to have to take one when we get back, so leave him be."

"Fine."

I kissed her once more, then got up to wake the boys.

Legend and King were both up when I opened the door. Legend was into his cell phone, while King was on his tablet playing a game.

"Morning fellas."

"Morning Saint," they both spoke.

"You guys are up early," I spoke as I walked inside.

"Papa is taking us fishing today," King beamed.

"I guess you're excited?"

"Yes sir."

"Me too. What about you, big man?" I asked Legend.

"I'm not all that excited. I don't want to touch those smelly fish."

I laughed and shook my head. Lately, I'd noticed that Legend was maturing. He was always on his phone, and he liked to look his best. My gut was telling me that a little girl somewhere was causing him to be that way. Only a female would make an immature young man act right.

"Well to be honest, I'm not all that excited either, but your papa wants to spend time with you."

"And question you," he smiled.

I shook my head yes, "Yes, that too. So I need you to be my wingman and help me out."

"I got you."

I dapped him up.

"I got you too, Saint," King added.

"I know you do, lil' man. Go ahead and get dressed. I'm going down to see what's for breakfast."

Consuela was standing up in front of the stove when I walked into the kitchen. Mr. Santana was sitting at the table reading the morning paper.

"Good morning," I spoke, getting their attention.

"Heaven's Saint," Mr. Santana chuckled. "How did you sleep?"

"I slept well, thanks for asking."

"Come catch a seat. Do you want coffee?"

"Nah, I'm not a coffee drinker."

"Breakfast is almost done, so we'll be eating in a little bit."

Mrs. Santana walked into the kitchen with Heaven close behind. They both spoke, then took their seats next to us. They boys were last to come down with their electronic devices in their hands. Heaven gave them both a look, and they sat the devices on the kitchen island. She didn't allow them to have them at the table, so she didn't have to say a word to them about it.

After breakfast, Mr. Santana gassed up the boat. The boys and I packed up all of the fishing equipment, and loaded it all on the boat. Heaven and Mrs. Santana were both on the back porch watching us. I smiled as I continued loading the boat. Once we had everything aboard, Consuela brought down some lunch that she packed for us. I loaded that on the boat, then helped King put on his life jacket. Legend didn't want to wear one, but Heaven wouldn't hear of it. Mr. Santana convinced him to put it on by saying that we were all wearing one.

We were finally off on the water. King and I sat at the front of the boat to catch the wind in our faces. Legend had his face planted in his phone that I'm sure was about to lose signal any time now. He thought he would be able to pass time by being on his phone, but he was in for a rude awakening. I looked back at him, and the look on his face told me that his phone was out of range. He looked up at me, so I waved him up front with us.

Mr. Santana finally found us a spot to fish in. King was excited as he ran toward the bait bucket. He couldn't wait to stick his hand inside and get a worm. Legend was still seated at the front of the boat looking.

"Legend," Mr. Santana called out. "Come on over here and let me show you how to bait your hook."

He made his way over as slow as possible, then grabbed his fishing pole. "Papa, I don't want to put my hand in there with those worms."

"Come on now, don't tell me you're one of those pretty boy types?" he joked.

"I just don't like creepy, crawly, slimy things on my hands."

"No way, you have Santana in your blood. We're not afraid to get down and dirty no matter how creepy it is. Come closer."

Legend looked over at me. I nodded my head for him to go. Mr. Santana saw it, and a smile spread across his face. I grabbed a pole for myself, then began baiting it. King had his baited, but was waiting for Legend before casting it out. I went ahead and threw mine out. It's been a while since I had fished. At first, I wasn't enthused about coming out, but now I'm looking forward to today.

While we waited for the fish to start biting, Mr. Santana was talking to Legend. He was talking low, but I could hear that he was asking about their father. Legend was being honest and answering all of his questions. Mr. Santana went from Flex to me. He told him that he liked me because I made his mother happy, and that I was giving them a little sister. *How vain*, I laughed to myself. I'm sure he had more reasons, but those must have been the most important.

"Look lil' man, something is on your line," I called out. I took my phone from my pocket to take some pictures of him.

"Yippy!" King jumped up.

"Alright now King," Mr. Santana said standing up. "Let's get that sucker."

King grabbed his pole and began to reel him in. He had the biggest smile on his face. I knew this would be a day that he would never forget.

"It's heavy, Papa."

"Okay, let me help you. Reel it in slow."

Mr. Santana placed his hands on top of King's, helping just a little. King was still doing the majority of the work. The fish hit the side of the boat, then revealed himself to us. It was a nice size fish, and he was flipping around everywhere.

"Whoa!" King smiled.

"That's a big fish, King," Legend congratulated him.

King pulled him inside and unhooked the fish himself. I knew he couldn't wait to get back to tell Heaven. I'm sure he couldn't wait to tell Flex either. I hope it made him feel bad that he missed this moment. If he wasn't a fucked up person, he would be sitting here instead of me. His loss was my gain, and I planned to be here for more first moments.

Mr. Santana and I both caught three fish apiece, while the boys had four. The sun was beginning to go down, so we packed up to head back. The boys sat up front talking about their fish, while I sat in the back with Mr. Santana. He called for me to come sit with him. I knew this day wouldn't go by without another conversation. Once he got the boat going, he looked over at me.

"It seems like the boys like you."

"I like them too. They are both great kids."

"Yes they are, and I want them to remain that way. I don't want them seeing any foolishness."

"I feel the same way, but I'm not there every time that their father comes by. I mean I've reasoned with him, I've kicked his ass, I don't know what else to do. Well, nothing that won't cause me to go to prison at least. But I don't want to do anything to their father, you know."

"I understand. I care about my family more than I do about him. But if he is a threat to my child, I have a problem with that."

"And so do I. Your child is carrying my child."

"You know, I never did like that guy," Mr. Santana grunted. "I warned Heaven about that loser."

Mr. Santana went on and on the entire way back about Flex. He was firing himself up without my assistance. His face was as red as a stop sign. I didn't try to interject or calm him down. I wanted him just as pissed off at Flex as I am.

CHAPTER 15

Heaven

The trip back home to South Carolina was much needed. I felt so rejuvenated on the plane ride back home. Saint seemed to enjoy himself with my family as well. He and the boys also got a lot closer on the trip. My mother and I did some shopping for baby things. This little girl did not know it, but she was set coming into the world. We bought so much that I had to send it home via UPS. I also got a chance to sit down with my father to discuss my situation with Flex. He put me in contact with one of his contacts in Dallas that specialized in child custody cases, and we were going to sit down for a meeting as soon as I got back.

"Did you drive yourself to the airport?" I asked Saint as the thought crossed my mind. I had completely forgotten to order a car service back home and I hated cabs.

"Yeah. I knew we would need a ride home."

"I totally forgot. I was dreading having to wait on a car service."

"You know I got you, babe," Saint kissed my hand. "I do need to talk to you about something. I wanted to talk to you on vacation, but we were having so much fun."

"What's on your mind?" I asked as my stomach dropped, because I did not have a clue what he wanted to talk about.

"I bought a house," Saint started. "I found it while we were apart. I did not know where our relationship was going and I could not keep living at Maw Maw's. I was hoping that you and the boys would move in with me."

I thought about what Saint was asking me. The last time that I tried living with a man it crashed and burned. I knew that I could not compare Flex to Saint because they were by far two different people. Saint had both the boys and my best interests at heart. My parents loved him as well. I do not know what was making me hesitate, but I pushed it to the back of my mind.

"I'll talk it over with the boys. If they like the idea…then I'd love to move in," I said, giving Saint an assuring smile. Saint kissed the back of my hand again. I could tell that he was a little disappointed in the answer, but it was not just me whose life was being uprooted. The boys would be affected also, and I always had to act in their best interest.

"I still want to take you to see the house once we land."

"I want to see it too. Knowing you…you got a shack somewhere," I laughed.

"You got jokes? Prepare to eat them words."

Once we landed and got our bags from baggage claim, Saint made me wait at the loading zone while he went to get his Suburban. I took the time to talk to the boys. I knew that we were going to ride by the new house, but I did not want to catch them off guard.

"Saint bought a house," I started the conversation.

"So are we moving to a new house?" King asked. Legend was too busy going through his phone. I knew that he was growing up, but I heavily monitored his Instagram account since that was the only social media he was allowed to have.

"I don't know…how do ya'll feel about moving in with Saint?"

"He's cool," Legend said, not looking up from his phone. "He spends the night almost every night at our house anyway, so what would be different?"

Legend was right. Saint had been spending a lot of time at our house, and the boys were used to him being around. I still wanted to see the house before I made any decisions. The location and everything mattered to me. I did not want to move too far out because I still had a job to go to, and the kids had to get to school.

I was surprised when Saint pulled into a neighborhood only about ten minutes away from my condo. It was a gated community and the houses were gorgeous. I was secretly in love with the location and when he pulled up to the house, I was even more in love. The boys were shouting with excitement. They kept asking if we were moving in and wanted to go inside.

"Do you want to see the inside?" Saint asked me.

"Yes, and the boys certainly do," I opened the car door and Saint rushed around to help me out.

He held my hand as we walked toward the door. I could hear

him fumbling with his keys. When he opened the door, I could see exactly why he bought the house. It was perfect. The open floor plan and dual master bedrooms sold me immediately. The boys ran through the house choosing which bedroom would be theirs. I had not even agreed to move in yet, but they loved the house. The backyard was also spectacular. There was a gated in-ground pool and a small basketball court with plenty of yard space to still have gatherings.

"I'm impressed," I smiled, looking up into Saint's eyes.

"I had you in mind when I bought the place. I just didn't know where our relationship was going."

"Well you did a great job picking it out. If the kids weren't here... well...we could break it in properly," I said, wrapping my arms around his neck and kissing him.

"So are you saying you're moving in?"

I kissed him deeply. "What does that say?"

"It says we're gonna have to add more bedrooms because Imma pump an ass of babies in you."

"Oh Lord," I laughed. "Take me home so I can thank you properly."

"We should grab some food on the way so we don't have to leave back out. A nigga got jet lag like a muthafucka."

"Sounds like a plan."

We loaded back up in the car. The kids talked animatedly the whole ride. They could not wait to move in and use the pool. I was not worried about them with the pool because I paid good money for them to have swimming lessons, so they were excellent swimmers. I wanted wings and fries, so we stopped at Wild Wings to get dinner. The boys fell asleep on the ride to the house. I was happy because when we pulled up to my house, something was definitely off.

"Why is my front door open?" I asked as Saint killed the engine.

"I don't know, wait here," he said, opening his trunk. I heard him move the suitcases around before he reappeared, heading toward the house with a gun in his hand. My heart immediately started to race.

After a few minutes, Saint came out of the house looking like he wanted to kill someone. I did not know what to make of his facial expression except whatever was in my house could not be good. I opened my car door and Saint immediately came to my side.

"You don't want to go in there."

"What's wrong with my house, Saint?"

"It's fucked up bad, babe."

"What do you mean? All this money I pay for security, there ain't no way someone got in my house!"

"The electric has been cut."

"The fuck you mean?"

"Chill, Heav. Don't let your blood pressure get up. You still carrying my baby."

"I want to see my house, Saint," I said, getting impatient. I started to say fuck him and this baby, but it would have been my anxiety talking and Saint was too crazy for some shit like that.

"Come on," Saint said, holding out his hand for me to take. I took hold and walked shakily to my front door.

It was obvious that the front door had been kicked in. What I did not understand is why the alarm company had not notified me. They were supposed to contact me as soon as something happened. The condo had a backup generator, so I used the light from my cell phone to cut it on. Once the lights were up and running, the severity of the damage hit me. The intruder completely trashed my house. They cut up my living room furniture and smashed my glass tables. My dining room table was destroyed. Upstairs, all of our bedrooms had been torn apart. Clothes were out of drawers and most of them had been stolen. My bedroom walls had been spray-painted with the words hoe, bitch, and slut. I was livid.

"The cameras," I seethed.

"What?" Saint asked confused.

"My place is wired with cameras. They are motion-activated all around the condo. Even though the power was cut, I should be able to see who cut it."

I pulled out my phone and started scrolling through the day's footage. I had been checking on my condo since I had been in Myrtle Beach, but I had not done it today because we were flying home and got side tracked going to see the new house. I finally pulled up the footage and scrolled to the end. They swore they were so smart cutting the power. They knew I had a hell of a security system, but they forgot about the camera. They also forgot to wear masks.

"I'm going to kill Kalina and Flex," I hissed.

CHAPTER 16

Saint

*H*eaven and the boys moved into my new house immediately. She was hesitant at first, but after the break in, she agreed with no problem. I knew that Flex had plenty of bitch in him, and that's why he waited until I left to come back and trash the place. I've tried my best to stay off his ass, but this was the last straw for me. I was sick of this hoe ass, worthless ass, bum ass nigga. For the life of me, I couldn't understand why the fuck he would destroy the possessions of his own children. How fucking selfish was that? That exposed to me how much bitchassness was really in his blood.

After two days, our new furniture was finally being delivered. We both got rid of all of our old furniture to start over together. I did keep the new bedroom set that I had recently purchased. Nothing was wrong with it, and I didn't want to sell it. I put it in the master guestroom. Heaven took the boys to play laser tag while everything was being moved in. I wanted to join, but I wasn't leaving anyone alone in my new spot. After the break-in, I really didn't trust anyone knowing where the new spot is. Jug was the only that knew right now, and only one other person needed to know—my grandmother.

I was in the office area setting up my desktop computer. Now that I had a nice home to work in, I would no longer be going to the office. That would be Manny's office to run from here on out. I decided just last night to make that decision. By working from home, I would be able to keep my baby when Heaven went back to work. I didn't want her going to daycare, so this would work out fine. The most I would be doing was consulting, and she could ride along with me to do that.

"Man, this crib is fat," I heard Jug say behind me.

"Thanks bro. What's good man?"

"Shit chillin'. Damn this house is bad."

"Come on, let me show you around."

I released the cords for the printer to go show him around the place. Jug had been my friend since forever, and he would be the first person to get a look. After we get everything situated, I would bring my grandmother by to see it. She had no idea that I was staying this close to her now, and I'm sure she would be ecstatic about it. I couldn't wait to see that expression on her face when she saw it.

"Where is Heaven?"

"She took the boys out for a while, they'll be back later on."

"What you gon' do about her baby daddy?"

"I don't know yet. The nigga ain't showed his face, so I ain't worried right now. I got to focus on one thing at a time, and right now my family being safe is my priority."

"I feel you. But just so you'll know, if I see that nigga I'mma

SHAMEKA JONES · VIRGO

handle him."

"Fine by me," I said, raising both of my hands up. "I don't give a fuck what you do to that nigga. If I see that nigga myself, it's on."

"I'm happy that you said that, 'cause I know where that nigga be at night. He fucks with this hoe that one of my homies used to fuck."

"Is the bitch named Kalina?"

"Yeah."

"Yeah, she used to be Heaven's friend. How much you think it will cost to send some youngins in there to fuck her shit up."

"Shit, young niggas will do that shit for free as long as they can get something out of it."

"I don't know what she has in her place that's valuable, but I got a G for whoever can get it done."

"Say no more, I'll hit the block and put the word out. You know niggas out here can't wait to eat, so it'll be done as soon as it gets out."

"Good lookin' out," I dapped him up. "Remind me to give you the money before you leave."

"Bet. You know I got to look out for my niece and my bro, right? This right here is some easy shit to handle."

We walked through the patio door, and out to the pool area. This was the part of the house that I loved the most. It was already beautiful out here, but I couldn't wait to put my final touches on it. The pool was a nice size and shape. I was going to add an infinity Jacuzzi, and a bricked waterfall to it. I also want to restructure the yard to add an in-ground trampoline. I'm sure the boys would love it, and baby girl that's on the way, for years to come.

After the furniture movers left, Jug and I retreated to the backyard to chill. We were sitting outside enjoying a bottle of beer when Heaven walked out. She walked over and took a seat on my lap. I rubbed my hand up her thigh, then rested it on her belly. It was growing so fast that it had me wondering if two were in there. I saw the sonogram for myself and there was one in there, but Lord God her belly was huge.

"Hey baby. Hey Jug."

"How you doing, Heaven?" Jug asked.

"I'm good. How about you?"

"Never felt better."

"Glad to hear that," she smiled. "What do you want for dinner, Saint? The boys want tacos."

"That sounds good to me."

"Okay. Are you staying for dinner, Jug?"

"Yeah, I'll kick it with you squares tonight."

Heaven laughed. "Alright. I'm going to go get started. Do you guys want another beer?"

"Yes. Thanks baby," I said, giving her a peck on the lips.

Just as she stood up to walk away, Legend walked out of the door.

"Good evening," he spoke. "What's up Jug?"

"What's good, big man. You lookin' fly as usual, lil' nigga."

"Stop callin' them niggas, nigga," I shot at him. No matter how many times I told Jug not to say that to them, he continued to say it.

Heaven and I weren't raising any niggas; we were raising young black men. I didn't trip about it though because Legend loved for Jug to be around. It was because he was so reckless with his words. I tried to refrain from talking a certain way in front of the boys. I had to lead by example. Kids learn from what you do, not from what you say.

"My bad bro. So big man tell me, do you have a lil' girlfriend yet?"

Legend blushed, then looked over at me. I kept a straight face as I looked back at him.

"I don't have a girlfriend yet, but I do like this girl in my class."

"What is it that you like about her?" I asked.

"She's smart, and she's pretty."

"Those are good qualities to start with. Tell me more about her."

"She's nice to me, sometimes she shares her hot fries with me during recess."

"That means she's not stingy," Jug added. "I like her already. You got to always make sure yo' lady isn't selfish. What's her name?"

"Aubrey."

"Aubrey? Is she white?" Jug asked.

Legend laughed. "No, she's black like you."

"You got jokes today? Well at least she's black. What her mama look like?"

We continued laughing and talking for another hour or so, until the food was ready. Jug and I picked Legend's brain about this girl that he thought was so cute. He had his first crush, and I wonder if Heaven knew. I'm sure she didn't or she would have said something to me about it. I didn't want to mention it to her because I wanted him to trust me with information. On the other hand, I couldn't keep secrets about her child away from her.

After dinner, I walked Jug out to his car. It wasn't late, but we had to get our house together. He wasn't trying to help, so he had to go. The kitchen needed to be cleaned, and all the beds needed linen. I promised Heaven that I would help, so chill time for me was over. The baby furniture had arrived also, and I was sure I would spend the rest of the night putting it together. That, I was actually looking forward to.

Legend's room was the first on the hallway upstairs. I stuck my head inside, and he already had his sheets and comforter on his bed. He was older, and he didn't need as much help as King. He was in his phone as usual, so I didn't say anything to him. I pulled the door closed halfway, then made my way down to King's room. Heaven was inside helping King make his bed. She smiled when she saw me.

"I'm gonna go get started on the baby's bed."

"Alright. I'm almost done here, so I'll tuck the boys in and I'll be down to help you."

"Okay. Goodnight King."

"Goodnight Saint."

I walked on down the hallway to our bedroom. I went through that and the bathroom to get to the nursery. All the boxes were posted up along the wall, so I grabbed the first one and got started.

Heaven walked into the room and sat down on the floor next to me. I was twisting the final screw in the bottom of the crib. I sat it up and took a look at it. It was started off right, but I had a long way to go. Heaven picked out a crib that has a changing table and a dresser attached. It looked to have a million pieces, but I wasn't going to sleep until it was put together.

"What are we naming this baby?" I asked, looking at her.

"I don't know," she replied, rubbing her belly. "What do you think?"

"Shit if I know. You did a good job with choosing Legend and King, so I trust any name you come up with."

"I got to think about it a little while longer."

"No rush, take your time and give her something pretty."

"I will."

"Did you know Legend had a crush on a girl named Aubrey?"

"No, who is she?"

"She's in his class. And she shares her snacks and shit with him."

"He told you about her?"

"Jug and I questioned him. Don't say anything because I don't what him to know I told you. Just ask him about girls and see what he tells you."

"I sure will. He is too young to be liking girls."

"A boy is never too young to like girls. He's about that age where he gets interesting instead of being disgusting."

"Oh my God. I'm not ready for my baby to grow up yet."

"Well there's nothing you can do to stop it, so you better get ready."

CHAPTER 17

Heaven

$\mathcal{I}$ told Saint that I needed to think more on a name, but I had already decided. I just did not want to tell him about it. It would be my little secret for a few more weeks. We had more pressing matters to attend to. Since my condo had been broken into, Saint and I had moved in together. I still had to figure out what I wanted to do with my condo. I finally settled on renting it out. I still owed a little on the mortgage and I did not want to sell it. If I rented it out, I could rent it a little higher than my mortgage and make profit.

"I don't think I want to go back to work after the baby," I said to Saint as we headed home following my doctor's appointment.

The boys were out with Vedra and Catana for the day. She would be bringing them home in a couple of hours. Since the break in, Saint was not crazy about everyone knowing where we lived, and I had to put my foot down about Tressa and Vedra. Kalina had left a really bad taste in his mouth about my choice in friends. I understood, but if he could hang with a knucklehead like Jug, I deserved Tressa and Vedra.

"The decision is up to you. I'll support whatever you do," Saint said, kissing the back of my hand.

"I'm serious. Don't say shit if all I want to do is invest money and not punch the clock."

"I trust you to be smart enough to not just sit on your ass."

I knew Saint was referring to Lailani when he made that remark, but I let it slide. Saint was just as damaged as I was, and I could not hold that against him.

"Never that playboy," I laughed.

"I know. I'd tell your daddy on you anyway."

"Don't think because you cool with my daddy he would take your side over mine. I'll always be daddy's little girl."

"Spoiled ass," Saint said, kissing my hand again.

When we pulled up to the house and there was a dark-colored sedan waiting along the curb, Saint's face darkened at the sight. He did not like unexpected visitors, and he damn sure did not like people knowing where we laid our heads. I guessed that was the street in him.

"Wait here," Saint said, getting out of the car. I did as I was told and watched the exchange between Saint and the middle aged white man that got out of the sedan. After a brief exchange, Saint returned to the car. "Come here Heav."

"Okay," I said with uncertainty. Saint helped me out of the car before walking with me over to the man.

"Miss Santana?" the balding man asked, holding his hand out to shake.

"That's me. And you are?" I asked.

"I'm Harold Epstein. Your father David hired me to represent you in your custody dispute."

"My dad told me he was going to reach out to a friend, but he did not say that he was hiring anyone," I said skeptically. "Are you any good, Mr. Epstein?"

"Do you think that your father would hire me if I weren't?" he answered back.

Touché, I thought. "I guess you're right. Well Mr. Epstein, we have about an hour before the boys come back. Would you like to sit and talk?"

"That would be best. I want to nail down a game plan."

Saint and I showed Mr. Epstein into the house. He laid out an aggressive approach to steering custody in my favor. If I had my way, I would have Flex signing over his rights. I even mentioned that to Harold, but he assured me to take one step at a time. He also assured me that the break in at my condo could also work in my favor. He did advise Saint to keep a cool head if he came into contact with Flex. I smirked because Saint got a kick out of whooping Flex's ass, but I also knew that Saint knew how important my kids were to me. Hell, if he had not straightened up, I would have been at the table talking to Mr. Epstein about his ass too.

Ж

I had finally been able to get the damages to my condo completely repaired and start showing it to potential tenants. I had placed an ad on Craigslist and was meeting the third person who had expressed an interest in leasing the condo. I was taking applications and thoroughly checking each applicant's background. I was about to turn over the keys to a very expensive condo, and was not about to do it to just anyone.

"Has he got there yet?" Tressa asked as I sat in my car waiting for the next potential tenant to pull up.

"No, but tell me about your date," I answered.

I had set her and Jug up on a blind date. Saint was against the idea of our friends dating, but Tressa was the only one of my friends without any male friends, and Jug needed some business. Saint was concerned about the fact that Tressa had three kids and Jug had none. Plus, he was not the most censored person around kids. I assured Saint that Tressa may be what Jug needed to calm his ass down, and one date would not hurt them.

"He showed up at my door with an ass of roses. Did that nigga get dating tips from Saint?" Tressa asked, and I started laughing.

"He coached him a little the day before."

"Well, Saint needs to go into business teaching these fuck boys how to treat a lady because Jug was a perfect gentleman. I just knew you was about to send me on a date with a nigga that was gonna be rapping at the table and asking the waiter if they served chicken wings."

"Girl, I would not do you like that."

"He's a good guy. We walked downtown after dinner and he held my hand. I was really shocked that he did not suggest getting a room."

"I told him don't treat you like a thot."

"Well thanks for the lookout. We're gonna go on another date."

"Well that's good," I said, noticing a car pulling in the driveway.

"Tressa, I'm gonna have to let you go. I think my future tenant just pulled up."

"Okay girl. Let me know how it goes."

"I will," I said, hanging up the phone.

I stepped out of the car and stopped in my tracks. The man getting out of the car was fucking gorgeous. I did not know if it was me or the hormones talking, but he stepped out of the car looking just like Chadwick Boseman from Captain America: Civil War, and I got weak in the knees. I swooned over his muscular arms and broad chest. I loved how they filled out his freshly pressed dress shirt. I wondered how he remained dry in the sweltering Dallas heat. I pulled myself together and straightened my sundress over my pregnant belly before I walked over to him with my hand out.

"Hi, I'm Heaven Santana. You must be Mr. Savoy?"

"Savoy is my first name," he said, taking my hand into both of his. I almost fainted. "My last name is Kinney."

"Okay Mr. Kinney, nice to meet you," I said, taking my hand back. I could feel my temperature rising.

"Likewise."

"Are you from the Dallas area?"

"No, I actually just moved down from Knoxville. I took a position as the head Engineering department at SMU."

"Impressive," I said. "Shall we take a look inside of the house?" I motioned toward the front door.

"Yes. It's a beautiful yard by the way."

"Thank you. My fiancé helped with the landscaping. There is also a basketball goal with a small blacktop," I said, using my key to open the front door. "The condo is four bedrooms, two and a half baths. The kitchen, living room, dining room, half bath, and an office are on the first floor."

Savoy walked through the first floor with me silently. Since the place was empty, my voice echoed off of the walls. I had forgotten how big the place was as we walked around to see the different areas. I led him through to the kitchen to let him take a look at the backyard. He was impressed with what Saint had done with the yard. I made a mental note to tell Saint about his good work. Upstairs, I showed him the three bedrooms and the hall bathroom before taking him into the master bedroom.

"The master bedroom has a walk-through closet with a large master bathroom," I explained, walking with him through the closet and into the bathroom.

"I see you had a vanity put in," he noted, seeing the custom vanity I had built in when I bought the condo.

"Yeah, but it is the perfect height to slide a laundry hamper under."

"This is a nice place."

"Yes. There is also an alarm system included in the rent. There is a backup generator in case of any power outages."

"You did a great job with this place."

"Thank you. If you're interested, you can fill out this application. It is a one-year lease term. The security deposit is $2000 as well as the rent. Security and first month's rent would be due at move in."

"Well if it's all the same, I would prefer to pay six months in advance."

"That would be perfectly fine with me," I said smiling. If Savoy's credentials checked out, he would be my number one choice to have as a tenant. It did not hurt that he was easy to look at. I just hoped that my looking would not land me in hot water with Saint.

CHAPTER 18

Saint

*I*t felt like the hottest day on Earth. I didn't know what the temperature was, but it had to be in the hundreds. It had been a while since I had been out here working, and I could tell. It was like I couldn't get enough water in my system or cool down. The good thing about it was that today was the last day on this job. This job has been one of the easiest, but they didn't have a lick of shade in their yard. Shade makes a great deal of a difference when you're outside all day.

Since we were pretty much done, I knocked on the door. I had half of my money up front, but I needed the rest today. Heaven had mentioned not going back to work, so I needed every penny that was owed to me. She had a good plan thought out, but I was going to be her backup plan. Most plan A's didn't work out exactly how we predicted them. I was taking every job that came our way to ensure we would be good. Baby girl wasn't even here yet, and she was putting a dent in my wallet. I wasn't complaining because she was the person that I was doing it for. Now that I would be responsible for a life, I was working ten times harder.

"Hello Saint," Mrs. Golden spoke as she opened the door.

"Good evening Mrs. Golden, is the Mr. available?"

"He's actually not in at the moment."

"Oh okay. Well we're pretty much done."

"Okay, here," she said, handing me an envelope. "He did leave this check here for you."

"Right on, that's what I was coming for. Do you want to come out and take a look at the yard? We're just about done with it."

"Sure, let me go get some shoes on."

I stepped back on the porch to wait for her. Mrs. Golden was an older lady, and she needed help getting down the stairs. She was excited about getting her new garden and rose bed, so I knew she would be happy with the results. I was a little more than impressed myself. These new guys were doing an awesome job so far.

After showing Mrs. Golden around, we packed the work truck back up. Mrs. Golden was happy with the results and so was I. Another satisfied customer to scratch off of the list. The Goldens were an older couple, so they hired us on full time to keep the yard up for them. I was happy about that because it would give me work all year around. I'd been lining up a few of my clients for year around work. Now that I had this huge family, I had to have a huge bank account to support them with.

"Alright guys, you all did good work today," I addressed the new crew.

"Thanks Saint," Kevin responded. Kevin was a rough neck that

Manny helped out a few years back. He had been getting into trouble since the age of ten, but Manny rescued him from it all.

"Tomorrow you guys can meet Manny over at his office. He will have a new job lined up for you."

"Now that's what I'm talkin' 'bout," Tremaine smiled. "More money in the bank." Tremaine, on the other hand, came from an abusive home. He was a foster child and would run away all of the time. Manny saw him one night digging in a dumpster and took him in without paperwork. He got on the right track and even graduated high school. College wasn't for everyone, so Manny hooked him up with this job. They were all enthused about making good money, and being able to take care of themselves financially. They have had a rough first half of life, but we were changing the rest of it for them. As long as they did what was required, they would have a job forever with me.

"I might not see you guys tomorrow because I will be in the office, but I will bring the checks out early Friday morning."

"Alright then," Kevin replied.

I dapped them up, then jumped into my ride.

Instead of going straight home after work, I headed over to my grandmother's house. It was still early, and I wanted to check up on her. Since I came back from South Carolina, I'd been mad busy. Now that things were beginning to settle down, I had some free time on my hands. I still hadn't told her about the house, so I would go ahead and spill the beans today. I was sure she would want to see it since it is right around the corner.

When I pulled up to my grandmother's house, there was a car in the driveway. The car was unfamiliar to me. I knew it was new from the paper tags that hung on the back. Not too many people visited my grandmother, so it was probably my mother's. I parked my truck alongside the curb and jumped out.

I could hear my mother's voice as soon as I entered the house. She was tickled pink about something. I made my way down the hallway toward the living room. When I walked into the living room, I was caught off guard. Lailani was sitting on the sofa next to my mother. My first thought was to turn around and walk out. I had to think about it for a split second. This is my grandmother's house, and I wasn't going to let her run me out of it. I scowled at my mother because I had already warned her about Lailani. She knew I didn't want her hanging around anymore. What if I would have come in with Heaven?

"Paw," my grandmother spoke. "How you doing baby?"

"I'm good Maw Maw," I spoke, but still eyeing my mother.

"Come take a seat. Are you hungry?"

"I am, but I will join you in the kitchen."

I helped my grandmother out of the car, and walked with her to the kitchen. I was highly pissed, so I didn't want to say a word to my mother. Lailani knew damn well not to even breathe too loud around me.

As soon as we hit the kitchen, my grandmother turned to look at me. She knew I was mad, and I know she is going to try to fix the situation.

"Paw, I don't know why Sharon brought that girl over here."

"Why does she hate me so much?"

"Aw Paw Paw, I don't think she hates you."

"Well why would she continue to do things that I tell her not to do to me?"

"Who knows Paw, I think she got that ADHD shit."

I laughed. "Maw, I'm serious."

"Hell, me too. We all know Sharon's elevator doesn't go up to the top floor. And whatever you tell her not to do, she sho' nuff will."

"I fuckin' hate her, man."

"Saint," she looked at me seriously. "Don't ever say that. Don't ever let me hear you say that again. She is your mother and you do not hate her."

"Maw-" I paused, then took a deep breath. "I just can't stand her is all. I can't."

"Well me neither, but that's my baby and she gave life to you."

"Yeah, and who says that's a good thing?"

My grandmother placed her fists on her hips. "I do, and I'm sure Heaven feels the same way. Now sit down and let me fix this plate."

"Yes ma'am."

My grandmother was the only person that I would listen to the first time around. She was the only person that didn't have to tell me twice. I never had to think about anything that she told me, because I knew it came from love. To me, she was superwoman and her apron was her cape.

After a light dinner, I walked back into the living room. My mother was still sitting there but I didn't see Lailani. I didn't know if she had left while I was eating or what. One thing was for sure, I wasn't going to ask about her. I took a seat on the opposite end of the sofa.

"Oh, stop being a baby Saint," my mother hissed at me.

"Stop doing irresponsible things, Sharon."

"Boy, don't make me cock back and slap yo' ass."

"You're not gonna slap him, Sharon," Maw Maw interjected. "I told you don't bring that damn girl back to my house, and Saint has asked you the same thing. Why can't you respect what this man is telling you?"

"'Cause I'm his mama, and I know what's best for him. That broad with all them fuckin' kids and that drama her baby daddy brings damn sure ain't what's best for him."

"Lailani is definitely not what's best for me. She fucked another nigga in my bed. I'd rather deal with some shit that's not in my own home than to deal with that. If that's what you will put up with, then that's you. I know what's best for me, and I don't need y'all making decisions for me. No disrespect, Maw Maw."

"None taken, baby."

"I was coming by here to take Maw to see my new house, but I'm not even in the mood anymore. Maw, I'll come by later to show you. Sharon, stay far away from me okay?" I said, standing up.

"So emotional," my mother laughed.

I didn't bother with a response because that is exactly what she

136

wanted. It was better if I said nothing at all anyway. I didn't want to disrespect my grandmother, but I would dig in my mother's shit at any given time.

The entire ride home, I rode in silence. I was trying to rearrange my mood before I made it home. I didn't want to have to tell Heaven about this bullshit. It would probably upset her and I didn't want to do that. We were in a happy place now that we are all settled in together. When I pulled into the driveway, Heaven's car was already parked. I sat there for a moment thinking about what I would tell her if she noticed my mood. It might as well be the truth since I was pissed.

"So this is where you live?"

I almost jumped out of my skin when I heard Lailani's voice behind me. I turned around, and she was in the third row of my Suburban.

"What the fuck, Lailani!"

"This is very nice, a real upgrade from the hood you had me living in." I put the truck in reverse and pulled out of the driveway. My blood was boiling now. If Lailani wasn't two rows back, I would choke the shit out of her. "Where are we going?"

"Why the fuck are you in my truck?"

"Because I want to talk to you. You never listen to me, and I wanted to get your attention."

"You can't get my attention Lailani, and this damn sure isn't the way."

"I'm sorry Saint, but I love you and I can't make it stop."

"I don't give a fuck. I done already told yo' muthafuckin' ass what is up, and you can't seem to get that through yo' fuck head."

I pulled right back up in front of my grandmother's house. By now, Lailani was making her way toward the first row of seats. I pulled the door open and grabbed her by her hair.

"Get the fuck out my shit."

"Saint!" she cried, holding onto her head as I pulled her out.

I grabbed her by her neck and pinned her against the truck. "Don't you ever in your natural life do that shit again. Next time, I'mma shoot yo' dumb ass." I pulled her off the truck by her neck, then jumped back inside.

She was standing outside of the truck crying her eyes out. I felt bad for doing her like that, but I would have felt worse if my piece was in my possession and I shot her. That shit alone ran me hot because that was putting my freedom at risk. This day was all fucked up, and I definitely wasn't going straight back home. I needed to clear my head, so I would take a ride around the city for a few hours.

CHAPTER 19

Heaven

I thought I had heard Saint's work truck pull in the driveway. When he did not come in the house after a few minutes, I checked the window and did not see him. I shrugged as I went back into the kitchen to start dinner. I had just finished going through the applications of my potential renters, and Savoy Kinney stood out as the best candidate. I called him to give him the good news. We made arrangements to do another walk through, collect payment, and sign the lease agreement. I also added that Saint could maintain the yard for him as well for an additional fee. I made a note to discuss it with Saint when he got home.

I checked the time and realized that Tressa and Jug would be over for dinner in a few hours. I had invited Tressa and the kids over so they could play in the pool, but once Jug got wind of her coming, he invited himself over. Vedra would be the only one missing from our gathering. She and her boyfriend had taken their kids on vacation to Disney World. They were getting serious, so they wanted to see how well their families blended. The boys were out back playing on the basketball court having the time of their lives. I picked up the phone to call Saint.

"Yeah?" he answered after a few rings.

"Are you okay?" I asked, taking the phone away from my ear because he answered with a serious attitude.

"Nah, I'm good."

"You don't sound good, babe."

"What is it, Heav?"

"I was calling you to remind you that Tressa and Jug were coming for dinner. Did you forget?" I asked. I heard him curse under his breath.

"I'm not in the mood for that tonight. Just cancel on them. I ate at Maw Maw's already."

"I can't cancel on them, Saint. Plus, I been doing all this cooking."

"All right. I'll be home in a little bit."

"Are you okay, Saint?"

"Yeah…we'll talk later. I love you Heav."

"I love you too babe."

I hung up the phone. Saint sounded upset. I did not know what had made him that way, but I damn sure wanted to find out. I hated when Saint got upset because he took it out on the people around him. There were only a handful of people that could get him out of character, but I was willing to bet his mother was at the root of this. I returned to cooking dinner when I was interrupted by a doorbell.

"Just a minute," I called as I checked on the ears of corn I had boiling on the stove. I wanted grilled corn, but Saint was not home to fire up the new grill he had bought and I had no idea how to work it.

I picked up my phone and headed to the front door. I was going to call Tressa and tell her to pick up the garlic bread that I had forgotten along with a bag of ice for the cooler. As I got closer to the door, I could see a female's silhouette. It was too early for Tressa to be here, so I figured it must have been one of our neighbors. I was sadly mistaken when I opened up the door to see Lailani.

"Is Saint here?" she asked, trying to look past me.

"No. How do you know where we live?"

"Saint brought me here before."

"Come again?" I raised an eyebrow. Saint made it clear on several occasions that he had no feelings for Lailani, so I did not understand why he was bringing her to our home.

"This was supposed to be my house," she said. I could hear her voice start to shake.

"Well…this should be a conversation you should be having with Saint," I said as I played with my phone, discreetly calling Saint. I tried to close the door.

"No," she said, putting her foot in the door so that I could not close it. "I'm having this conversation with you. You got pregnant to trap him, didn't you? Why can't you just let him go and let us be happy?"

I looked at this bitch like she had lost her mind. It was bad enough that I had to deal with Kalina's crazy ass, but to throw Lailani in the mix was too much.

"You could not have been too happy with Saint if you were riding another nigga in the bed ya'll used to share."

141

"That was a mistake!"

"So what? You slipped and landed on a nigga's dick? Twice?"

"I was lonely!"

"Well you're super lonely now. I do want to thank you for fucking over Saint the way you did though, because I would not have had the pleasure of loving him."

"You don't love him! You just want his money!"

"Unlike you, Lailani...I have my own money. Saint could leave me tomorrow and I would not skip a beat. I would survive and be able to take care of all three of my kids," I smirked, placing my hand on my round baby.

"It's probably not his baby anyway. Saint and I were together for years and never had kids. Why are you pregnant after a few months?"

"Why is it your problem? God saw fit for Saint and I to bring a life into this world. I don't question Him."

"Whatever," she sucked her teeth. I was getting tired of having this conversation. I did not know how Lailani found out where we lived, and I definitely was not happy about it.

"I'm going to ask you to leave now," I said calmly. "My king and I have guests coming, and your presence is not wanted."

"I'm not going anywhere until I speak to Saint!"

"Baby girl, if Saint wanted to talk to you...he would have reached out and touched you."

"I'm not going anywhere."

"Don't make me get my gun, Lailani," I warned. I hated that it had to come to this. I had not even told Saint I had a weapons permit, but since the phone was on the secret was out.

Lailani opened her mouth to speak, but she was interrupted by the sound of screeching tires. I looked over her shoulder and noticed Saint jumping out of his truck. His face masked in anger, he marched to the door. I was actually scared for Lailani. Saint looked like he wanted to choke her to death. I wanted to step in between them and try to save her, but then again it was not my fight. I saw how Saint handled men when he was angry, and a small part of me wondered how he handled women.

"The fuck you doing here, Lani?" he seethed.

"How can you just throw me away, Saint? Throw us away?" she said, trying to lay her hands on his chest. He brushed them away.

"You threw yourself away when you couldn't keep your legs closed. You need to leave before I call the law on you."

I knew he meant it. Saint did not fuck with the police, but it had to be something serious if he threatened to call them on Lailani. I watched her as her face changed from sad to angry. She used her small hands and started pounding him on his chest. Saint grabbed her by the wrists and shook her a little.

"Lani...I'm not fucking with you," he said through gritted teeth.

"Why don't you tell Heaven how you brought me over here in your truck, but left because she was here!" she yelled.

"Stop playing," he chuckled. "You know you hid your ass in my backseat on some stalker shit."

I guess Lailani yelled that shit out to piss me off. The only thing she succeeded at was letting me know she was a messy ass bitch. That was the difference between Saint and I. I was not so quick to believe what came out of someone else's mouth. Plus, Saint knew I was bound to be at home anyway since I was not working. He would not disrespect our home by bringing someone else in it. That was the shit Lailani would do. I grew tired of watching their exchange, so I stepped back into the house to take my lasagna out of the over and took the time to call 911. I explained to the operator that my fiancé's ex-girlfriend was at our home causing a commotion and would not leave the property. After giving her my address, I knew that Dallas PD would be here in no time since the neighborhood was full of doctors and lawyers.

"Who was that?" Saint asked. He startled me because I did not hear him close the door on Lailani. I could still hear her beating on the door and yelling. I hoped that the boys did not hear the commotion.

"I called the cops," I said, shrugging my shoulders.

"Good, because if I stayed out there any longer, she would end up with a dotted eye. I had to push her out the door when she tried to come in."

"You wouldn't hit her for real?"

"If she kept trying to throw jabs like she was Mayweather…hell yeah."

CRASH!

Saint and I turned in the direction of the noise. He started back out the door, but I grabbed him by the arm.

"Don't," I warned. "Whatever it is…we have insurance to fix it."

"She has a death wish."

"Well I don't want you sending her to the upper room. You gotta be out here to help me with this little diva," I smiled, placing his hand on my stomach.

I watched as Saint's shoulders relaxed. There was another crash, followed by the sound of sirens. Saint and I got to the window in time to see the officers take one of the large stones that lined our walkway from Lailani. We watched as they placed her in cuffs before we opened the front door and stepped out on the porch.

"We need to get a statement from you, if you don't mind," a female officer stated, stepping onto the porch. She pulled out a pad and began to scribble a few words.

The officer took our statements and made notes on the damage that Lailani had done to my windshield and Saint's passenger window. I regretted not pulling my car into the garage when I looked at the shattered glass. Saint shook the officer's hand as she handed him the police report that we would need to file with our insurance company. The police called a tow truck to impound Lailani's car. We did not go back into the house until we watched the patrol car pull off with Lailani in the back with her head hanging down.

"Well that was fun," I said sarcastically and smiled.

"About as fun as a root canal," Saint said, wrapping his arm around my shoulder and kissing my forehead.

CHAPTER 20

Saint

For the past few days, I'd been trying to wrap my head around all of the bullshit. Lailani crossed the line by coming to my house the other day. I hated the fact that she knew where we laid our heads now. I hoped the police held her dumb ass for a minute. She didn't do anything too serious for them to keep her, so I'm sure she was back out on the streets. That bitch was so crazy that she wasted her one phone call on me. She was starting to become a problem again, and I wasn't going to deal with it. I filed a restraining order against Lailani, which was something I never thought I would do. Neither Heaven nor myself were scared of her, but I needed a paper trail just in case I end up hurting that bitch. By any means, I would protect myself and my family from whomever.

I sat in my office for hours setting up appointments and consultations. After what happened the other day, I was staying close to home. Heaven was off of work, and I wasn't going to leave her here alone. Lailani was on some other shit, so I had no idea where her head is. She wanted everything that Heaven had now, and she was extremely jealous of it. She was trying her best to mess up what we had. If only she had put that much effort into our relationship, we would have still been together. At the same time, I was glad she didn't because I wouldn't have met my Heaven Santana.

When I emerged from the office, the house was quiet. I walked through the house heading toward the kitchen. As I passed the patio door, I saw Legend and King in the backyard. They were jumping on the trampoline that I installed yesterday. I was glad that they were taking a liking to it so my work wouldn't go in vain. I grabbed an apple out of the fruit basket and rinsed it off. I stood there watching the boys doing back flips as I ate my apple. It reminded me of Jug and I when we were little boys. The difference was we were flipping in the grass with nothing to catch us if we did it wrong.

I made my way up the stairs and into our bedroom. Heaven was lying across the bed in her bra and panties. She was always hot now, even though it was cold as hell in this house. I eased closer to her quietly, then rubbed my hand across her thigh. She took a deep breath but was still sleeping. I rubbed my hand over her belly, then down inside of her panties. Heaven opened her eyes and looked up at me smiling. I pushed her legs open, then slid her underwear down.

With no hesitation, I went down to lick Heaven's treasure box. She sucked her teeth, then let out a long moan. I pushed her legs open wider as I stuck my tongue inside of her tunnel. She held the back of my head as she began moving her hips. I slid my tongue across her clit, then sucked softly.

"Shit," she whined.

"Cum all over my face."

"Fuck daddy. I am," she whispered while I sucked her clit; I flicked my tongue over it. I felt her body shaking, so I know her climax was near. "Don't stop, Saint."

Her body shook again, then she began to try to close her legs. I knew she was there, and I wanted to get there also. I stood up and pulled my pants down. She laid there smiling in anticipation. I pulled her by her ankles to the edge of the bed. I leaned over her belly and placed a kiss on her lips. While we kissed, I slid my muscle over her pussy, then pushed it inside.

"Mmm," I moaned.

"Oh, that feels so good Saint."

"Mm-hmm, I love the way you feel around me. Damn."

"Fuck me Saint."

I threw her legs over my shoulders and began thrusting faster. We had to make this a quickie since the boys were outside. Heaven held my arms as I brought us closer to ecstasy. Her pussy began pulsating, bring my soldiers out of hiding.

"Shit Saint, I'm cummin'."

"Me too baby, me too. Fuck."

In one last thrust, I exploded inside of her. I pulled out, then sucked the nut back out her of pussy. Her body shook and she giggled. I went to the bathroom to clean my mouth, and got a towel to wipe her up.

After my nut, I went down to check on the boys. They were sitting on the patio in the chairs. When I opened the door, they both turned to me. They were looking bored now.

"Can we go swimming?" King asked.

"Sure, why not."

"Yay," he screaming, jumping out of his chair. They both ran inside to change into their trunks. It's been a while since I had swam, so I went back inside to change also. I told Heaven what we were doing, and she wanted to put some meat on the grill. Since we canceled on Jug and Tressa the other night, I told her to go ahead and invite them over. We could enjoy ourselves with the kids this evening.

I got the grill started while Heaven prepared the meat. The boys were already running in and out of the pool doing cannon balls. They loved this pool already, but it would be way better when I finished it. I hadn't had a chance to add the additions to the pool yet. I'd be starting on that project tomorrow. Once I was done, we could throw a little gathering here to show it off.

"Here you go, baby," Heaven said, handing me the pan of meat.

I took it from her then pulled her closer to me. "Give me a kiss." She leaned in to kiss me and I grabbed a hand full of her ass. "I want some more of that later."

"You know you don't even have to ask," she flirted.

I looked over at the boys in the pool. "Girl, you better get that fat ass on up out of here before I get you."

She laughed as she walked away. I stood there watching her ass jiggle under the wrap she had around in her bathing suit. Man, I couldn't get enough of that woman. It was time for me to start making plans to make us one. I knew I wanted to marry her, there was no doubt in my mind about that; but before I could ask, I had to get her father's blessing. I wouldn't dare ask that man's daughter to marry me without his approval. He seemed to like me, but I didn't really know.

While the meat was on the grill, I jumped in the pool with the boys. They were playing Marco Polo, so I joined in. Since I joined in last, I had to be Marco. They were good swimmers, so it was hard for me to catch them at first. Once I realized that they were huddled up in the deep end, it was on. It didn't take me but a few strokes to catch them once they started kicking and splashing, trying to get away.

Tressa's three kids came running out of the house with their towels. Jug was behind them with bags in his hand. I laughed to myself inside as I watched him being a family man. I had never seen Jug actively playing stepdad to anyone's children. It was definitely a good look for him after the things he had done.

"What's up boy?" I spoke as I climbed out of the pool.

"You got it bro. I see you gettin' ya swim on and shit."

"Yeah man, I ain't been swimming in forever."

"Me either. I gotta hit this bitch too."

"Already. Let me get over here and check on this meat real quick."

I dried my hands off then went to check on the grill. The meat was halfway done, so I flipped it on the other side. Tressa came walking out of the house with a pitcher of margaritas in her hand.

"Hey Saint," she spoke.

"Hey Tressa, how you doing?"

"I'm doing fine, Saint. Thank you for inviting us over."

"No problem."

"Those kids were on our nerves in that house. This will sure enough tire them out."

"Anytime. I'm sure the boys will be in the pool all summer, so whenever they want to swim, bring them over."

"You might regret saying that," she laughed.

"Nah, it's all good."

When I checked on the grill the second time, the meat was done; I grabbed the foil pan and pulled it off of the grill. Heaven was inside finishing up the last of the side dishes.

"I was going to set everything up out," Heaven spoke.

"Oh okay. You need help bringing the rest stuff out?"

"Yes please."

"Alright, let me take this out."

I picked up the bowl of potato salad on my way back out. Heaven made the best potato salad, and I couldn't wait to dig into it.

Of course, the kids weren't ready to eat, so the adults sat around the table eating. This gave us privacy to talk about what happened the other day. I gave Jug a briefing on what happened, but I hadn't had a chance to go into any details. The entire time I was telling the story, Jug was giving me that *I told you so* look. Jug was with me the night I met Lailani, and he kept telling me not to mess with her. I was so caught up in her beauty and fat ass that I couldn't see past it. We had some fun times together, but I still regret the day I met Lailani. I wouldn't have if she didn't turn out to be a crazy ass stalker bitch.

After dinner, Jug and I took a walk out in the yard. We always had to have our private talks away from the ladies. It wasn't like we were keeping secrets or anything; it was just a man thing. I was showing him where and what I was going to add to the yard.

"I wanted to talk to you about that bruh," Jug spoke.

"About what?"

"Hookin' a brother with a job. Now that I'm with Tressa, I can't be out here hustling in these streets."

"So you're ready to go all the way legit?"

"Yeah you know, if the pay is right."

"Don't worry about that pay, that's gon' be on point. Just make sure you're ready to work, no bullshittin'."

"I am."

"Alright 'cause I don't have a problem with firing yo' ass," he laughed. "You can start by helping me with the yard, then we'll get you out there with the rest of the crew next week."

"Bet that. Good lookin' out, bro."

"I got you."

"And that other thing you asked about is taking care of."

"No doubt."

I finished showing him around the yard, then brought him back to the pool. I wanted to give him an idea of what we were going to be doing to it. Jug had never done work like this, so I was going to teach him everything hands on. I had faith that my boy would become great, and I would give him his own company eventually. Once he proved that he was ready to get on the right track, the sky was the limit with my company. I could have my company and two sub companies under me. That would ensure that my family was secure for years to come.

CHAPTER 21

Heaven

It was the day that Flex would be served with court papers. Mr. Epstein recommended that I file for full legal custody with a child support agreement. I agreed. Flex had been living the easy life since I had the kids, and it needed to stop. Since he wanted to be a smart ass and threaten me with taking my kids, I was going to hit first—and hit hard. I had a private investigator to pull up all the dirt that he could on Flex, so if he wanted to jump stupid in the courtroom, I had his number. Mr. Epstein assured me that if Flex knew what was good for him, he would agree to the terms without an issue. I, on the other hand, knew that Flex was not that bright, and he would assume that he could talk his way out of it.

"What time is Epstein supposed to call?" Saint asked me as I sat on our patio watching him and Jug work in the yard.

"Any moment now. The papers were supposed to be served this afternoon."

"You good?"

"Yeah," I said, flipping my phone over in my hand. I was ready to get this over with.

Once the gauntlet was dropped, I knew there would be no turning back. Flex needed to assume responsibility for our kids. I spent the better part of a decade taking care of them with very little help from Flex. If it were not for his mother, I do not think that Flex would have stepped up at all. It was like he checked out after I got pregnant with King. It was cool though, because he was in for a rude awakening. I was tired of doing this on my own. Even though Saint helped out, it was not his job. My phone vibrated in my hand; I knew it was a text because it only did it once. I already had an idea of who it was because Mr. Epstein was older and texting was not his thing.

FLEX: *You real funny. You think you gonna keep my kids living with that ex-con?*

HEAVEN: *Just because you haven't been caught doesn't make you any better.*

FLEX: *If this is how you want to play Heav...you don't want to go up against me.*

HEAVEN: *I'm not gonna entertain this conversation any longer. See you in court.*

I sent the text message and called Mr. Epstein. Saint was still working in the yard, so he was not paying me any attention. Surprisingly, I was not bothered by any of the drama that was going on in our lives.

"Heaven, I was just about to call you," Mr. Epstein answered the phone. "I just got word that your kids' father was served the custody papers. I petitioned the court for a hearing to grant temporary full custody to you as a formality. We want to do things right and have everything on paper because if we don't, he can just take the kids and not give them back."

"I understand," I nodded, even though he couldn't see me through the phone.

"I will be in touch with you in a few days to let you know about the court date, and if you need to appear."

"Okay," I said. "Thank you, Mr. Epstein."

"No problem, Miss Santana."

I hung up the phone to see several Facebook notifications. I really needed to block Kalina, but the nosiness in me would not bring myself to do it. I opened Facebook to see that she had posted pictures of the papers that Flex was served. I laughed because she was making a case that her man was a good father, and I was solely after his money. I wanted to respond, but I knew that it would not be in my best interest to do so. I would just sit quietly and watch the both of them hang themselves.

"What you looking at?" Vedra asked me from over my shoulder. I had forgot that she was coming over to help me think of a theme for the nursery.

"Flex got served his custody and child support papers today. Kalina is showing out on Facebook."

"I hope you're not feeding into her."

"Nah...I'm just lurking."

"If I were you, I'd screen shot everything."

"I am," I said, taking a screen shot of Kalina's thread.

"Let's go look at this nursery," Vedra said, going back in the house.

"Saint!" I called out, standing from my seat.

"Yeah babe?" Saint said, looking up while shading his eyes from the sun.

"I'm going inside with Vedra. The papers got delivered."

"You cool?"

"Yeah it's cool. I'll be inside if you need me," I smiled and went in the house.

Tressa was supposed to come over after Quan's 7 on 7 football game. She and Jug had really been hitting it off and they were starting to get serious. Her kids loved him. He was so hands on with Quan and football. The girls had even grown on him. He had cleaned his language up a whole lot since he had been around them. I was happy to see Tressa finally hitting it off with someone. At one point, Vedra was the only one of us that had a serious relationship going on. Now, we could all take a couple's vacation together once I had baby girl.

Vedra and I went through a few magazines picking out themes that I liked and pinning them to the wall. Since Saint had already set up the furniture, it made it a lot easier to see how the colors would blend with the furniture. I loved purple and I had found a lavender and cream layette that I loved. Vedra turned her nose up at it, but started to come around when I talked about adding gold accents. I had just settled on which accents I wanted to add when Tressa arrived. She liked the whole set up. Happy with my decision, I started placing orders online for the items I needed to bring the whole room together.

"You spent how much?" Saint damn near yelled when I told him how much I had spent later that night.

"Relax babe," I said. "It's not that much, and it will last for a couple of years."

I placed my hand on his thigh and moved to his hardening muscle. I knew that a few licks from my tongue and a little deep throat action would take his mind off of the money I spent. Saint was acting like we were hurting for money when we both had pretty hefty bank accounts. I guessed that me not going back to work was getting to him as well; the stress of having a family was probably starting to be a lot of pressure on him as well. It was my job to relieve that pressure and help him relax, so I took him in my mouth.

"Don't think because you sucking my dick that I'm…damn Heav," he gasped, forgetting what he was saying.

"What were you saying?" I smiled wickedly as I came up for air. Saint did not respond. He just placed his hand on the back of my head and guided me back onto his throbbing dick.

I sucked him like I had a hoover living in my jaws. Saint ran his hand through my hair as I bobbed up and down on his shaft. As I sped up my pace, he lightly wrapped my hair around hit fist. It turned me on so much that I started to salivate, making it extra nasty. I was happy that is was late at night and the boys' rooms were down the hall, because I knew that a simple act of giving head would turn into all night love making. My sex drive had been crazy since I had been pregnant, and Saint was more than happy to oblige anytime I needed him. He had the stamina of a horse.

"Shit Heaven," he huffed as he finally released his seed down my throat.

I swallowed him up and licked my lips. I stood to go brush my teeth, but Saint had other plans as he pulled me back onto the bed. I giggled as he parted my thighs and nibbled on my clit through my panties. I squirmed as Saint held onto my thighs and ripped my panties from my body to get better access to my goodies. He was like a kid in a candy store as he ate me up. I orgasmed twice before he released my thighs. His face was soaking wet as he kissed me so that I could taste my own sweetness. I was so busy relishing in the taste of my juices on his lips that it took me by surprise when Saint slid into me.

"Fuck," I whispered, biting down on his lip as he grinded slowly inside of me.

"Shhhh...just enjoy it," Saint whispered as he kissed me again.

My eyes rolled in the back of my head as he continued to make slow love to me. I heard a faint buzzing and thought that I had gone temporarily deaf from the pleasure, until I realized that it was my phone ringing. I lifted my head to see my phone was lighting up on my nightstand.

"Ignore it," Saint said as he kissed me, and I closed my eyes in submission. It was short-lived as Saint's phone started lighting up on the opposite nightstand.

"We need to get that," I whispered.

Reluctantly, Saint pulled out of me and rolled over to get his phone. It had just stopped ringing when he looked at the screen. My phone immediately started to vibrate again. I reached over and quickly answered it.

"Hello?" I answered.

"Miss Santana?" Savoy's deep voice spoke from the other end.

"Yes, what is it Mr. Kinney?"

"I'm sorry to call so late, but there has been an incident at the condo and the police wanted to speak with you."

"Why? What happened?"

"It seems as if your alarm was tripped by someone throwing a brick through the downstairs window. They need to verify that I am the tenant here."

"Did they catch who did it?"

"No ma'am. They think because it's the summer, it was probably some teens acting out."

"Okay. Can you put them on the phone please? It's pretty late and I don't want to wake the kids to come out," I asked. I also knew that Saint would not let me go alone.

"Sure thing. One moment," Savoy said. There was a brief silence before an officer took the call. He advised me that he would be leaving the police report with Savoy so that I could file it with my home insurance company. I thanked the officer, but I swore that my life was becoming a series of court orders and police reports.

"I will be out first thing in the morning to have the window repaired. There is some plywood in the storage room if you want board it up for the night," I said once Savoy got back on the phone.

"Thank you. I'm sorry for disturbing you so late, I just thought that this would be something that you needed to know about right away."

"Thank you for calling me, Mr. Kinney. I'll see you in the morning."

I hung up with Savoy and filled Saint in on the details. Saint also thought that maybe it was a group of teens acting out, but I was not as convinced. The whole situation felt like something Kalina or Flex would do as payback for putting him up for child support. I wanted to check the cameras right away to get to the bottom of it, but Saint assured me that even if it were them, he would take care of it. I did not know what he meant by that, but something in his eyes told me that I did not want to know. He kissed me deeply before climbing on top of me again. This was no time to be thinking about sex, but Saint was determined to get my mind off of the night's events and relieve some stress. After a few strokes, his plan was definitely working.

CHAPTER 22

Saint

*J*ug came over early this morning, so he jumped in the truck with me. It was Friday and I had to take the guys their checks. With morning traffic, it was going to take a few hours. The crew was split up in two different locations, so it would take longer than normal. I promised them that I would always bring their checks early, and I was a man of my word.

"You'll get to meet all of the guys today. I'll let you choose which crew you want to work with."

"Who do you usually work with?"

"I don't go out too much now to work, but I've worked with both."

"Are they cool?"

"Yeah. Most of them are young, but they are just like us. They came up rough, and trying to make it you know."

"I got you."

"I'll come out with you for a few weeks though. Just to make sure everything is running smooth and you got your job down."

"Good lookin' out."

I took the next exit and made a left.

When I pulled up to the first site, I could see the guys already working. I drove up alongside the curb and shut off the engine. Jug and I both jumped out as Manny made his way towards the truck.

"What's going on boss man?" Manny spoke.

"It's all good, boss man," Manny smiled. He was so used to be being the boss that he hadn't realized he was one as well. "This here is my boy Jug. Jug, this is my main man Manny."

"What's up," Jug dapped him up.

"You got it, bro."

"Jug here will be joinin' the crew Monday."

"Alright then. We can use some more help."

"He still needs a little training, but I'll be out here to help him along. Here are the checks," I said, handing him the checks for everyone on his crew.

"Good deal."

"I have to get over to the other site, so I'll see y'all on Monday."

Jug, Manny, and I dapped each other up, then we were out.

After dropping the checks off at the second site, Jug and I went back to my house. We went out to the backyard to put the final touches on the pool. Jug is a fast learner, and it didn't take long to train him. He still had some growing to do, but he was headed in the right direction. It looked like a completely different pool from a week ago. The Jacuzzi was installed, and now we were adding the bricks for the waterfall. I didn't want to mess up the yard by driving a forklift through it, so we were moving the bricks by hand. That added more time to the job, but it was well worth it.

"Damn it's hot out here," Jug complained.

"Shit, don't I know it; but you will get used to it."

"How do you get used to hell?"

"I don't think about it. I concentrate on completing the job."

"All I can think about is my damn back burnin'."

"Nigga, get you some sun block and stop complaining. You've only been working a week, it's too early to be complaining."

"My black ass don't be wearin' no sunblock."

"If you don't want your shit burnt you will."

"I got you."

"Come on. Let's get this last brick into place."

We both bent our knees to pick the slab up. It was heavier than the other bricks, and had to be carefully placed on top. If it ended up with a crack in it, we wouldn't be able to use it. It had to be perfect in order for the water to flow correctly.

After the last brick was placed on top, we stood back to admire our work. The yard turned out just the way I wanted it to. We added a few trees for shade, a rose bush, and a small garden in the far back. I was going to grow some vegetables on my own. Instead of buying from the supermarket with all those pesticides on them, I wanted to take a stab at growing fresh veggies. With all of the hormones that they pump into animals, I had a mind to get a few chickens, pigs, and cows. I'm sure Heaven wouldn't go for that, but it was just a thought. I myself wasn't going to take care of any animals anyway.

"Hit the switch, Jug," I called out.

"I got you."

I wanted to make sure that the water flowed right. If there were any problems, we needed to know about them now. When Jug flipped the switch, all the lights came on then the water began to flow.

"Hell yeah," Jug smiled.

"We did it bro," I said, dapping him up.

"This shit is freaky as fuck. We need to put one of these in the back of my yard."

"What, a pool?"

"All of the above. It's not as big as your yard, but I want a pool and waterfall of my own."

"To be honest, with all the work ahead of you, we wouldn't be able to do it until it gets cool outside."

"That's fine, I'm not in a rush. Plus, we can just use your pool until then," he laughed.

"I'm not trippin'. You know whatever is mine is yours."

"Already brother."

"This is beautiful," Heaven called out from behind us.

I turned around smiling. She had an even bigger smile on her face.

"You like it baby?" I asked.

"I love it. It is amazing."

"Wait until you see it at night," Jug spoke. "It's gonna look ten times better."

"I can't wait. Saint, I'm going to go pick the boys up. Do you need anything while I'm out?"

"No, I'm good. If I'm gone when you get back, I'll be over Maw Maw's."

"Okay, is she alright?"

"Yeah, I got to go pick up and drop off her medicines."

"Alright, maybe we'll stop by on our way home."

"Yes, do that. Maw Maw has asked why you haven't been by to visit."

"You didn't tell me that. I'll be by there."

"Okay, see you later," I said, giving her a kiss on the cheek.

"Bye baby, bye Jug."

"Alright now, Heav."

"You can turn it off now, Jug."

Once I paid Jug and he left, I took me a quick shower. I was so hot that I end up taking a cold shower. Since I was just going by the pharmacy and my grandmother's, I threw on some cargo shorts and a white t-shirt. It was a simple outfit, so I put on a necklace and a watch to go with it. I sprayed on a few drops of my Versace cologne before heading out.

By the time I made it to my grandmother's house, Heaven's car was already out front. I didn't see my mother's car, and that was a good thing. Heaven wasn't too fond of her, so I didn't want them around each other alone. Since the whole situation with Lailani, my mother hadn't been around anyway. I know she had something to do with her hiding in my car that day. Lailani rode with her over to my grandmother's house, so she knew that she wasn't gone. I'm not one hundred percent sure, but she probably put it in her head to come back by the house. Lailani wasn't that insane, and after I choked her up I'm sure she would have stayed away.

I could hear Heaven laughing and my grandmother talking when I entered the house. That sound alone warmed my heart. The two women I cared about the most were getting along well. I also smelled food being cooked, so I'm sure we would be staying for dinner. That would work out perfectly, and it left us with a clean kitchen at home. I'm sure Heaven would appreciate it also.

"Hey Paw."

"Good evening Maw Maw," I said, leaning over to kiss her cheek.

"You hungry?"

"Always. Where the boys?" I asked Heaven.

"They are out in the back."

"Oh okay. Kevin from the job gave me some Six Flags tickets today. Do you want to take the boys with them?"

"Sure, I wanted to take them to do something else before the summer ends anyway."

"Cool. I gave Jug some as well, so we'll make it a family day."

"Do you have any for Vedra? I don't want to keep leaving her out."

"I do," I smiled.

"Let me go check on the food," Maw Maw said, rising from the chair.

I sat her medicines on the coffee table, and took a seat next to Heaven. Her face was glowing something serious and it was beautiful. I placed my hand on her belly to feel the baby. She was always moving around, and it was amazing to me. It looked like it hurt, but Heaven said it didn't.

Dinner was ready so we all washed up. I was starving and ready to fill my belly. Like always, my grandmother made me lead the prayer.

"Father God, we come to you today giving thanks. Thank you for the many blessing you have bestowed upon us. Thank you for the food, thank you for the love around this table, and most of all thank you for family. Bless this food and the person who prepared it. We love and appreciate you, in Jesus name we pray. Amen."

"Amen," they all said in unison.

My grandmother sat back and smiled as everyone began to dig in. That was where most of her happiness comes from—feeding people good food. I was sure if I could cook like her, I would find happiness watching other people enjoy my food as well.

"Maw Maw, we finally got the house and the yard together. When do you want to come by?"

"Whenever you come get me."

"I can take you tonight. I'm ready to see what the lights and waterfall look like at night."

"We have a waterfall?" King asked in excitement.

"Yes, and guess what?"

"What?"

"I made it so that you will be able to jump off of it."

"Can we go swimming tonight?" Legend asked.

"I don't know, you have to ask mama."

"Mama, can we?" King begged.

"Why would you put that off of me, Saint?" I held my hands up and smiled. "Not tonight, boys. You need to rest so that we can go to Six Flags tomorrow."

"We're going to Six Flags? No way," King bounced in his chair.

"Yes, and everyone is going."

"Even Quan?"

"Even Quan," she laughed.

"I can't wait," Legend smiled.

Heaven looked at me and sighed in relief. I knew I put it on her to answer about swimming, but that was because I wasn't going to stay out and watch them. I was already tired from working all day, and I would just fall asleep on them. Even though they were good swimmers, we didn't let them swim without supervision.

After we finished dinner, I stayed and helped my grandmother clean the kitchen back up. Heaven wanted to get the boys ready for bed, so they went on ahead of us. She was always sleepy, and I knew it is more or less her being ready for bed. I didn't blame her; I was ready to hit the sack myself. I was going to give Maw Maw a quick tour and bring her back home.

Once the kitchen was clean, we jumped into my truck and headed over to the house. When we made it the boys were still up, but they had showers already. I showed my grandmother the guest bedroom first. I let her know it was hers anytime she didn't want to be home alone. Heaven had decorated it just for her. Maw Maw loved it and said once the baby comes, she would be spending plenty of nights.

I opened the patio door and let Maw Maw walk out first.

"Oh my God, Saint. This is amazing."

"Thanks."

"You did this all by yourself?"

"No, Jug helped me."

"Jug? You mean to tell me that boy knows how to do something with his hands other than steal?"

I laughed. "Yeah. He is trying to turn his life around too."

"Seeing you doing well must have made something click in his mind."

"A little of that, and the fact that he has a good woman now."

"Oh, that's what it is. Well a good woman will make the worst man want to do right."

"I agree."

"I'm proud of you, Saint. You have really turned into a man. Now when are you gonna make an honest woman of our Heaven?"

"I've been thinking about it. I have to talk to her mother and father first though."

"Well at least it's on your mind."

"Of course," I smiled and wrapped my arm around her shoulder. We stood there and looked out over the yard that was lit up. Jug was right; it did look ten times better at night.

CHAPTER 23

Heaven

*I*t was too hot to be walking around Six Flags as pregnant as I was. I was 30 weeks and ready to pop. I was miserable, and I was faking like everything was okay. I knew that it would probably be one of the last times this summer that I would be able to do something fun with the boys. I would have preferred a waterpark since I was unable to ride the rides with everyone, but I was determined to stick it out.

"How you feeling, big mama?" Vedra asked, hanging back to keep me company. All of the boys were making a beeline toward the Superman ride.

"Yeah," I said, placing my hands on my back. "I really want a frozen lemonade."

"It is hot out here. We'll go find one when they get in line. It'll give us time to sit and rest."

"Is Tressa riding?"

"Girl yeah," Vedra laughed. "You don't see her up there leading the way?"

"I don't blame her because I would be right up there with her."

"I'll still be the one holding the bags because I'm not getting on that," Vedra laughed. "I ain't never died before. I don't want to try it now."

I was relieved when we finally made it to the ride and saw that there was a Coldstone stand right next to it. I told everyone to meet us there when they were done. Saint could see the discomfort on my face and looked torn about riding the ride. I told him that I was fine and someone needed to stay with the boys. He finally relented and kissed me on the forehead before Vedra and I headed off to sit in the shade and eat ice cream.

"So how are things with you and Stephan?" I asked Vee.

Vedra was a freelance photographer for the Dallas Morning News. She met Stephan when she was asked to photograph him for a news story the paper was putting together on him. He was a lot like Saint and Jug. Stephan grew up in the West Dallas projects with his single mother. They were extremely poor, and sometimes he ran drug packages for local drug dealers to help his mother with bills, and to keep food on the table. He managed to keep himself under the radar and still get an education. By the time he graduated, Stephan was offered a partial scholarship to The University of Texas. The dealers he worked for helped to pay for the remaining tuition. Stephan was able to parlay his business degree and subsequent master's to head one of Dallas' top consulting firms. If you ever watched House of Lies, this translated into Stephan being one of the best bullshit artists in Dallas.

"They're going. He's been mentioning marriage a lot," Vedra said, picking at her ice cream.

"So…that's a good thing right?"

"I guess…but my last marriage wasn't nothing to write home about."

"At least you have a last marriage. I can't even get a first."

"Girl please! Saint is going to ask you. You can see it in his eyes that he loves you. It's only a matter of time."

"I doubt it. We got too much stuff going on. Besides, that house is in his name. He could put us out whenever he's ready," I pouted.

"Stop being all dramatic. If Saint was not serious about you, he would not be building this life with you and your kids. Flex fucked you up so bad that you're waiting for the rug to be pulled from under you. Trust me…Saint is in it for the long haul."

I sat back and thought about what Vedra was saying to me. She was right, but I hated to admit it. One of our exes was bound to drive us apart. I just had the feeling. Vedra and Tressa kept assuring me that they would beat a bitch ass before that would happen. I was lucky to have friends like them as opposed to Kalina. I was not always worried about some random chick running up on us in public because they were sleeping with her man. It used to happen all the time with Kalina. It was embarrassing as hell.

"That was fun," Tressa beamed, taking a seat at our table. Her hair was all over the place. I tried to brush it down for her as she took a bite of my ice cream.

"Ummm, you don't steal food from a pregnant lady," I said, taking my spoon from her.

"Jug is getting mine," Tressa whined. "I couldn't wait."

I looked over my shoulder and saw all the men in line with the kids. I smiled because none of these men had kids of their own, but they accepted ours. It took a real man to do some shit like that. We were some lucky ass women. They were some lucky ass men too though. We all had our own jobs and money, so it was not like we were after theirs.

"Tana really likes Stephan," Tressa pointed out to Vedra. Catana was holding Stephan's hand pointing out the toppings she wanted on her ice cream.

"Yeah," Vedra said, looking on. "He's really good with her. He's the first male figure she's ever had in her life."

"What about her father?" I asked. I knew that Vedra had been married before, but she never talked about her ex-husband. I just knew I never saw him around.

"He's in San Antonio with his new family. Cason left me when I was pregnant with her."

"I hate niggas like that," Tressa spat.

"I don't sweat it. He never held a full-time job down, and I was supporting us. I'm actually better off without him."

"I hear that," I said. "I feel the same about Flex. Saint is the complete opposite of Flex."

"Speaking of your sorry ass baby daddy," Tressa pointed at me. "When is your court date?"

"At the end of the month," I answered, cleaning my cup of ice cream and wondering if Saint would get me another.

The judge had granted temporary full custody to me. Flex was only able to see the boys one day a week at his mother's house. She would do the picking up and dropping off as I requested limited contact with Flex. The judge was reluctant at first, but when I showed him the screenshots and text messages that he and Kalina had been sending me, he got on board quick. Mr. Epstein assured me that this was all a step in the right direction, and temporary custody would lead to full custody. He did mention that the lawyer that Flex had procured was very underhanded and would probably try to drag me through the mud. He told me that with everything the private investigator I hired had dug up on him, we should still be in good shape.

"Let us know the date and time," Tressa said. "We want to be there."

"I will. My parents are coming down too. I had to talk my dad out of wanting to sit second chair. He loves a good fight."

"I heard your dad was a beast in the courtroom," Vedra said.

"He does what he can. I just don't want him fighting my battles."

Our conversation was interrupted when the fellas came and sat around the table with us. They had settled the kids around their own table, and we sat in the shade enjoying our ice cream. After a few "pleases" and pouty faces, Saint finally got me another cup of ice cream. He was dead set on me eating healthy during my pregnancy, but I reminded him that I was going to be walking around in the hot sun all day and he broke down. Saint rubbed my back while we sat and took a break. The kids finished their ice cream quickly and were ready to go get back on rides. I had to remind them that they needed to let their treats settle for a few minutes so that they would not get sick on the rides. The boys thought it would be funny to vomit on someone from the ride. The girls did not find it funny. We decided to do a few kiddie rides while they waited on the ice cream to settle in the stomachs.

"You feeling okay?" Saint asked me, taking my hand as he walked me through the park. We looked like the typical cheesy couple that went to the amusement parks and matched. We both had on denim shorts and white tees with matching Air Maxes; so did the boys. I found some cute maternity shorts that still fit like the short shorts that I loved to wear.

"Yeah," I smiled. "The ice cream break helped. I can at least get on the merry go round."

"Awww the baby gotta ride the baby rides," he teased, and I hit him in the shoulder.

We stayed at the park until it was close to closing time. The kids were all complaining about being hungry as we walked to our cars. It was still pretty early, so we decided to stop for dinner as a group. Everybody wanted something different, but we eventually settled on Chili's. I was famished and wanted everything I saw on the menu. Saint was trying to reel me in, but I was like a kid in a candy store. I ordered appetizers and a dessert. All he could do was shake his head. I was eating for two, and what my little mama wanted she was going to get.

"I think I have heartburn," I said, rubbing the space between my breasts. I could feel the acid building in my throat.

"I tried to tell you not to eat all that shit," Saint said, giving me the side eye.

"I wanted it. I'll just take some acid reflux medicine when we get home."

"Should you be taking that with my daughter still baking?"

"Baking? Boy, this is not a potato. It's fine. The doctor prescribed it."

"Okay," Saint said, placing his hand on my thigh. He knew that was one of my spots.

If the boys had not been in the car, I would have had my head in his lap as we cruised down I-30. Saint just brought out the freak in me, pregnant or not. I believed it was because we loved to please each other in the bedroom. Saint was more concerned about me getting mine than him getting his. That was the main difference between him and Flex. Flex would bust off of head and roll over to go to sleep. It always baffled me why I never cheated on him. I guess I was just loyal and stupid. Saint always made sure I came three or more times before he went for his first nut. Even after that, he would not be through with me. Our love making usually lasted well into the morning. I was glad I was no longer working because I was never any good after Saint put it down on me. I just know that my man left me satisfied, and I hoped that he would propose soon so he could satisfy me for the rest of our lives.

CHAPTER 24

Saint

*I*t has been more than a month of Sundays since I last went to church. My grandmother has been pressuring me to come with her every week for the past month. Today, I decided to join her since she is singing a solo. Heaven was getting her snore on, so I didn't bother waking her up. Since I was attending the 8 o'clock service, I might make it back before she even woke up. I moved quietly around the room gathering my things.

When I walked out of the bedroom, I could hear that the boys were up. I walked down the hallway toward their rooms. Legend's door was opened, so I walked inside of his first.

"Morning big man."

"Hey, good morning Saint."

"What are you doing up so early?"

"I don't know," he smiled.

King ran into Legend's room and jumped up on the bed.

"Morning lil man."

"Good morning Saint," he replied, jumping in the bed.

"Where are you going?" Legend asked.

"To church with Maw Maw."

"I want to go also."

"Do you?" He shook his head yes. I looked down at my watch and we had plenty of time. "Well go find you something nice to put on."

"Me too?" King asked.

"Yeah you too, and don't get too loud. I don't want to wake your mother up."

"Okay," King smiled, jumping off of the bed.

"And stop jumping in these beds, boy."

They ran off to get dressed, and I went to put the finishing touches on myself.

Fifteen minutes later, the boys came running down the stairs. I was in the kitchen grabbing a few things to snack on. We don't have time to stop and pick up anything to eat, so this would have to hold us until service was over. I threw it all in a bag, then turned to look at the boys. They did a great job of dressing themselves.

"Saint, can you show me how to tie this tie?" Legend asked.

"Sure, come on over."

I wrapped the tie around his neck, and proceeded to show and tell him how to tie it. King stood next to us attentively watching my every move. He had a clip on tie, but I would buy him a real one and show him how to lie it later.

As soon as we jumped in the truck, my grandmother called. I told her we were pulling out of the driveway. She was already at the church even though it didn't start for another 30 minutes. We should make it there with at least five minutes to spare. I know she wanted me there early to sit up front, but I didn't want a VIP seat. I was fine with sitting somewhere in the middle or the back. I'd let the regulars have those seats.

"Fellas, let me ask you something," I said, looking through the rearview mirror at them. "How do you feel about your mother and me getting married?"

"I'm okay with it," Legend spoke.

"Me too. So does that mean you are our father now?" King inquired.

"I will be your stepfather, yes. Your father will always be your father."

"I like you being our father better," King spoke honestly. "You play with us more. We have fun when we are with you."

"Well," I said, then paused. I didn't even know how to respond to him. "We're going to continue to have fun. Okay?"

"Okay."

"I have to call your Papa to see if it is okay with him to marry your mother."

"I think he will be okay with it too," Legend spoke. "He likes you even though he doesn't act like it."

"You think so?"

"Yes. He smiled at you, and he never smiled at our dad."

"We will see."

When we pulled up to Progressive Baptist Church, the parking lot was full. Maybe my grandmother was right about warning me to get there early. The boys were finishing up their snacks just as I found a spot. I grabbed a granola bar and an apple from the bag. I scarfed that down, then opened my door. Since the child proof lock was on, I had to let the boys out. I looked them over to make sure their clothes were clean before heading toward the church.

After we were ushered to our seat, the choir stood up to sing. Looks like we made it in the nick of time. Maw Maw walked up to the front and began to lead to choir. I closed my eyes and listened to her beautiful voice. Maw Maw sang around the house, but she put her all into it when she sang in public. It had been a while since I had heard her singing anything. I loved hearing it, so I lived in the moment.

I saw my mother walking toward the front of the church. Right behind her was Lailani. Usually I would be upset with my mother, but today I wasn't going to give it any energy. I closed my eyes and began to pray. I prayed that Lailani would stay away, far away from me and let me live my life. Never had I asked God for that favor, so I was hoping he would grant me this one wish. I just wanted to live happily ever after with Heaven, and I didn't want any interference.

When service was over, I was trying my best to get us out of the church quickly. Maw Maw scoped me out in the crowd, and called me over. She began to reintroduce me to all these people that I didn't remember. I was embarrassed about not coming in a while. That was one of the main reasons I was trying to make a great escape. If I didn't have the boys with me, I would have made it out.

"They are having lunch in the back, do you want to join us?" Maw Maw asked.

"No. We left Heaven at home sleep, but I'm sure she's up by now."

"Why didn't she come along?"

"She didn't know I was coming. She still looked tired from walking around the park yesterday, and I wanted to let her rest. Since the boys were up, I brought them along with me."

"Alright then. I'm glad you came by and brought the boys with you."

"Sure thing, I'll stop by later on to check on you."

"Okay Saint. Bye boys."

"Bye Maw Maw," they both waved.

I took a look around the church as I made my way out. Neither my mother nor Lailani were in sight, so I grabbed the boys and ushered them out. I wasn't in the mood to see or talk either one of them. All we had to do now was make it through the parking lot.

The coast was clear on the outside, and we were on our way home. I had two missed calls from Heaven that I had to return. She was a little upset that we didn't wake her up this morning. When I mentioned bringing her some food home, that mood flew straight out the window. Food always did the trick to steer Heaven's mind into a different direction. She wanted Olive Garden, so I called to place an order for everyone. Today, we were going to chill and relax at home.

Heaven said that she was going to go the Redbox and pick up a few movies to watch.

After pulling back up at home, I sent the boys inside with the food. I still needed to make that call to Mr. Santana, and I felt the need to do it today. I hadn't purchased a ring just yet, but with his blessings my search would start tomorrow. Nervously, I scrolled through my phone until I came upon his number. I pressed call and waited for him to answer.

"This is David Santana."

"Hello Mr. Santana, this is Saint."

"Oh, how are you Saint?"

"I'm great sir, thanks for asking. How are you and the Mrs. on this lovely day?"

"We are well. Is everything alright out there?"

"Yes sir. I'm calling because I'm ready to commit the rest of my life to your daughter. I want to ask for your blessing to ask her to marry me."

He was quiet for a second. "Of course you have my blessing, son."

I sighed in relief, not just because he gave me his blessing, but because he called me son. I hadn't had a father figure in my life since my grandfather passed, and it almost felt weird. I have never had any male to call me son though; this was a first.

"Thank you so much, Mr. Santana."

"You're welcome, and you may as well get used to calling me Pops," he laughed.

"Sure thing."

"Make sure you take care of my daughter, and grandchildren."

"No doubt about it. When are you guys coming to visit us? We have a room waiting for you."

"We will come out that way soon. Once I have everything in order here."

"I look forward to it. I'm gonna go inside now, please don't make mention of it to Heaven, I want it to be a surprise."

"I won't, and I'll make sure Jubilee makes no mention if it as well."

"Thank you so much. Goodbye."

Now that I had that out of the way, it was time to start looking for a ring. Maybe I could get Vedra or Tressa to help me out a little. I didn't know Heav's ring size, nor the type of rings she liked. I didn't know if she preferred gold over platinum, or what cut of the diamonds she liked. I'm sure they would be more than happy to help me with it.

"Hey baby," I said, giving Heaven a kiss.

"You guys looked nice today. I hate that I missed the service."

"I didn't want to wake you, you looked worn out."

"I was. I am glad that you let me sleep in."

"See, I was looking out for you."

"Whatever," she laughed. "Go get changed, I'll set up the food and get the movie ready."

Since we were lounging around the house for the remainder of the day, I threw on some basketball short and a t-shirt. When I made it to the family room, Heaven had the boy's food set up on the floor on some TV trays. They had thick blankets surrounding them to lay on afterward. She had our food set up in front of the sofa. I sat down next to her and began digging in.

Once we were all full, Heaven put the movie on. The first movie was Fantastic Four. It was a family friendly movie that we could watch together. I didn't mind watching it one bit because I loved the first two. Heaven and I cuddle up on the sofa with the blankets over us; I was glad they were, because I was able to feel all over her. I didn't like to do it in front of the boys, so this was perfect. She was just as frisky as I was because she began to rub all over me. My body was beginning to grow hot, and I was trying my best not to drag her up the stairs. I wanted her more than anything right now, but I held my composure. Right now, I wanted to enjoy the movie with the boys. Once they drifted off, which I knew would happen, I would be waxing that ass.

CHAPTER 25

Heaven

$\mathscr{I}$ was nervous walking into the courtroom. Saint and my mother kept trying to assure me that there was nothing to worry about. My father remained solemn, as if he were standing beside the bed of a sick friend. I did not know how to take it because my father was usually so reassuring. My mother told me that he was always like that before a big case, and I had nothing to worry about. I wanted her to tell that to my stomach because it was aching due to the anticipation.

When we entered the courtroom, Flex was seated with his lawyer. Kalina was sitting directly behind him. She was really taking the girlfriend role seriously. I looked forward and walked through the swinging divider that separated the people involved in the court proceedings from the onlookers. I took a seat next to Mr. Epstein, who was in deep conversation with my father. They looked to be going over case files. As much as I wanted to tell my father to butt out, I was happy that he was lending a hand.

"How are you feeling, Heaven?" Mr. Epstein looked up, noticing me sitting next to him.

"I'm okay. My stomach is a little upset."

"It's just the jitters," he smiled. "Your father used to break out in cold sweats before big cases."

"It will be fine, sweetie," my father said, patting my shoulder.

I nodded my head and stared at my hands. I could see Kalina shooting dirty looks at me out of the corner of my eye, but I would not fully focus my attention on her. Instead, I focused on my manicure. Saint had not come into the courtroom at the same time as me, so I started to get nervous. His presence always seems to calm me, but without him, the dull ache in my gut persisted. I just hoped that he came into the room soon before court started. A few moments later, I heard the courtroom door open. I looked back to see Saint enter, followed by Tressa and Vedra. I could not help the huge smile that spread across my face.

"You know we were not going to let you go through this and not be there for you," Vedra said, hugging me around my neck.

"We told you to tell us the day and time," Tressa said, taking her turn to hug me.

"I know. I was just so nervous."

"For what? Girl, you are a great mother," Vedra waved me off. "The judge would be blind not to see it."

"Is that Kalina?" Tressa asked in a hushed tone. She moved her eyes in Kalina's direction.

"Yes girl," I rolled my own eyes.

Tressa opened her mouth to say something else, but was quieted by the bailiff calling the room to order. He introduced the Honorable Janet Kaan before she instructed that we may be seated. Judge Kaan read off the court docket, and Flex shot an evil glare in my direction. I took a deep breath and faced forward. Judge Kaan asked for both lawyers to approach. Mr. Epstein gave me a reassuring smile as he walked toward the bench. I looked behind me and Saint mouthed that he loved me. I turned in time to see Mr. Epstein return to our table.

"Ms. Santana, I see that you are petitioning the court for sole custody of the minor children. Is that correct?" Judge Kaan asked me.

"Yes your honor," I spoke in a pained tone as a wave of discomfort washed over me.

"Any request on visitation?" the judge asked while making notes.

"Yes your honor," Mr. Epstein spoke up. "Ms. Santana is willing to give Mr. Brooks every other weekend and two weeks out of the summer. Mr. Brooks will not be allowed to take the children out of the country."

I could hear Flex scoff. I thought I was being more than generous. If I had my way, I would have mandated that he could not take my children out of the state. Flex had proven on more than one occasion that he was not the most responsible person when it came to dealing with our kids.

"What does the father request?"

"He wants joint custody your honor, and to dismiss the child support request," Flex's lawyer spoke up, and I did not flinch. I was glad that I had maintained my composure because the judge focused her attention on me. She was probably trying to gauge my reaction.

"Am I to understand that both parties have character witnesses?"

"Yes your honor," both attorneys spoke at once.

I looked around and noticed that Kalina was the only person sitting on Flex's side. That's when it dawned on me that Ms. Peggy was missing. I did not have long to wonder where she was because the judge was calling Kalina to the stand. I watched as Kalina strutted to the stand in a dress that looked like it was an entire size too small for her. I watched as the judge swore her in, and she kept her eyes on me the entire time.

"She used to be my best friend," I whispered to Mr. Epstein.

"Not to worry," he assured me.

I watched as Flex's lawyer tried to paint him as father of the year using Kalina as Picasso. She testified that Flex was a good father that saw his kids every time he had a chance. She also testified that he provided financially for them. I sat back and watched Kalina hang herself as well as Flex. I was surprised that their lawyer did not advise them of the receipts for clothing purchases and logs that I kept of when Flex gave me money, and how much was given. By the time Kalina left the stand, Flex had the smuggest look on his face.

Mr. Epstein decimated Kalina on the stand. He called into question her own character and motive for testifying against someone she once called a friend. Kalina started to stutter on the stand. I watched intently as the judge scribbled her own notes. Mr. Epstein shocked me because he was so mild mannered every time that we met, but he was acting like a rabid pit bull as he questioned Kalina. I almost felt sorry for her as she stepped down from the stand. She mouthed the word 'sorry' to Flex as he sat back in his seat with a clear look of disappointment on his face.

"Is that all from Mr. Brooks' character witness list?" Judge Kaan asked.

"Yes your honor," his lawyer answered.

"Mr. Epstein...you may present your first witness."

The uncomfortable feeling in my gut came back. I shifted in my seat to get comfortable. I watched as each of my witnesses were called and questioned. They held up nicely as Flex's lawyer tried to break them. When Saint was called to the stand, his criminal history was brought into question. It was also the first time that I saw the judge frown. My stomach tightened back into knots. I loved Saint, but I hoped that his background did not cause me to lose my boys. Mr. Epstein was able to spin Saint's background by acknowledging how he had turned his life around. The judge seemed impressed that he was able to turn his life around and build a successful landscaping business. I beamed with pride because Saint had overcome a lot of obstacles to get to where he was.

After my parents had testified, it was time for Flex and I to speak. The judge called me to the stand first. I was shaking, and my stomach seemed to knot up even more. Baby girl was moving as if she were performing gymnastics inside of my womb. The bailiff helped step up on the stand and swore me in. I smiled timidly at the judge as Flex's lawyer stood first.

"Good afternoon," he said. I smiled tightly at him. "Ms. Santana, have you ever kept your children from their father?"

I knew he was going to lead with that question. I wondered which cereal box Flex got his information from.

"Yes," I answered into the microphone.

"Why would you do something like that if you are such a good mother?"

I opened my mouth to answer, but a sharp pain shot through my abdomen. It was not the dull knotting sensation that I had been experiencing for the day, but it felt like someone had just stabbed me and twisted the knife. I took a deep breath and tried to will the pain away.

"Please answer the question," the judge instructed.

I gathered myself. "I have kept the boys away from Mr. Brooks when he has exhibited violent behavior toward me."

"Isn't it true that your boyfriend, Mr. Mitchell, has physically assaulted Mr. Brooks before?"

"Yes. Mr. Brooks was the aggressor…" I started to speak, but he cut me off.

"A simple yes is fine. In fact, Mr. Mitchell has attacked Mr. Brooks on several occasions. Is this correct?"

"Yes," I said tightly, rubbing my baby bump.

"So how can we trust your judgment?"

"Because I love my boys. If I did not feel safe around Mr. Mitchell, I would not bring my kids around him."

"I see…no further questions," the lawyer said before returning to his seat.

Mr. Epstein stood from his seat with a slight smile on his face. "There was an incident at Dave and Buster's. Can you explain what happened?"

"Yes sir," I smiled as another pain ran through my body. "Mr.

Brooks was angry that I was out with another man. When Mr. Mitchell tried to diffuse the situation, Mr. Brooks struck him."

"Was he with his current *girlfriend*?"

"No sir, he was with another female."

"Does Mr. Brooks have steady relationships?"

"Not that I know of. I have never seen a female last longer than a few months."

"Objection!" Flex's lawyer shouted. "Relevance?"

"It pertains to the defendant's character," Mr. Epstein explained.

"Overruled," Jude Kaan said. I could tell that she did not care too much for Flex or his attorney. It was like she could detect bullshit.

"Ms. Santana, you previously stated that Mr. Brooks got violent with you," Mr. Epstein said pointing towards Flex. "Can you please elaborate?"

"Yes…" I was halted by another sharp pain and the sudden urge to pee.

I grabbed my stomach and I began to panic because I knew it was too early for me to be in labor. I was only 34 weeks. The pain hit me again like someone was stabbing me repeatedly. I looked up at Saint and could see the worry in his eyes. I did not want to alarm anyone, but the pain made me want to scream out. I took a few deep breaths and the pain subsided.

"Are you okay, Ms. Santana?" the judge asked me.

"I'm fine. Do you mind if I get a drink of water?"

"We will take a ten-minute recess," the judge said instead.

I stood from the witness stand and immediately stopped in my tracks. The judge and everyone else focused their attention on me. I stood wide-eyed for a moment because I thought my mind was playing tricks on me. I thought maybe I peed on myself. It was not until the sharp pain hit my body again that I took it for what it was worth.

"Are you okay, Ms. Santana?" Judge Kaan asked again, sounding concerned. Saint was already making his way toward me.

"My water just broke your honor," I said, looking down at the small puddle that formed between my feet.

TO BE CONTINUED

Looking for a publishing home?

Royalty Publishing House, Where the Royals reside, is accepting submissions for writers in the urban fiction genre. If you're interested, submit the first 3-4 chapters with your synopsis to submissions@royaltypublishinghouse.com.

Check out our website for more information: www.royaltypublishinghouse.com.

Text ROYALTY to 42828 to join our mailing list!

To submit a manuscript for our review, email us at
submissions@royaltypublishinghouse.com

Text RPHCHRISTIAN to 22828 for our
CHRISTIAN ROMANCE novels!

Text RPHROMANCE to 22828 for our
INTERRACIAL ROMANCE novels!

Do You Like CELEBRITY GOSSIP?

Check Out QUEEN DYNASTY!
Visit Our Site: www.thequeendynasty.com

Get LiT!

Download the LiT eReader app today and enjoy exclusive content, free books, and more